PRINT ISBN 978-0-9998314-6-5

❀ Created with Vellum

USA TODAY BESTSELLING AUTHOR

ALISHA KLAPHEKE

BAND
of
BREAKERS

To the noble ladies of fantasy

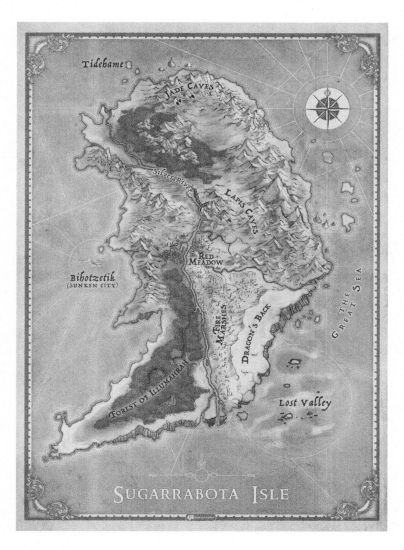

SUGARRABOTA ISLE

CHAPTER ONE

I n the dead of night, the Lapis library was as silent as a
tomb.

A high fever had struck Vahly down, and they'd
been forced to stay with Amona for over a week. But the
hallucinatory dreams and violent dizziness did nothing to
dispel the strange urge inside Vahly, the bone-shaking
urgency her magic thrummed through her body. With every
heartbeat, her magic demanded that she travel to the
western mountains. Now. Immediately. Before it was too
late.

Too late for what? Vahly didn't know.

The fever had abated, and the night of their departure
was here.

Finally, Vahly could give in to that insistent drumming
in her veins and rush toward the mystery of what her magic
sought. She couldn't leave fast enough to suit her.

Arc theorized that Vahly's new magic had caused the
fever, but it didn't matter now. They had magic to follow
and sea folk to overcome. And no one knew how much

1

time they had left before the flooding started and the end began.

The western coast was such an odd destination, a place where humans had once flourished and now only sun-faded art, flooded streets, and castles eaten away by time remained. Her mother Amona had taken her there a long time ago—to the lands above the great city the Sea Queen had flooded in one of her first efforts to cover the world in water—but Vahly had been too young to process the gravity and history of the place. Vahly pressed a hand against her chest, the magic pushing, pushing, pushing. No, the fever didn't matter and neither did the strange quest. It simply had to be done.

The silence in the Lapis caves dragged a distinctly creepy feeling down her spine. The library was always quiet, but not like this, not this deep sort of silence. Usually, a youngling wailed from somewhere inside the labyrinth of tunnels and rooms, and oftentimes, dragons of mating age would stay up late drinking and teasing one another.

But tonight—nothing.

She really hoped the grave-like stillness wasn't an omen for their quest to see the scant ruins and caves above the sunken human city of Bihotzetik.

What if the fever had been a warning? A counterbalance to her need to get into the western mountains?

Exhaling her stress, she held up a lantern. The light painted Amona's blue-scaled hands as the Lapis dragon matriarch pushed a bookshelf away from the northeastern wall of the library to reveal a round, wooden door in the rock wall, a brass knob glinting from its center.

The door squeaked open under Vahly's hand. "I had no idea this was here."

Amona donned a half-smile. "I'm allowed some secrets, Daughter. Listen, I'll keep an ear to the ground and contact you if I hear of anyone following you or if any intend to harm you."

Nix stood beside Arc, a pack slung over one shoulder and wing. The black of her pupils nearly overcame the bright yellow of her irises. "Why would anyone want to ruin the one chance we have against the Sea Queen?"

Arc had a scroll open on the table beyond the secret door. He probably hadn't even noticed the door or Amona's words. Absently tapping his bottom lip with his thumb, he squinted at what appeared to be a list of dragon herbal remedies, complete with colored drawings of green leaves, purple stems, and white blooms. As an elf with royal blood, his vision was exceptional, far better than Vahly's or any dragon's. The squinting and thumb tapping were simply his *thinking* pose.

Amona handed Vahly a bag of what smelled like fresh bread. Amona had insisted on seeing them off herself, with no one else around to preserve their lie that Vahly and the others were closeted in meetings about the coming war and her new powers. Amona had said none needed to know that Vahly's earth magic was still rather limited. Fear would only complicate things and dampen the hope Vahly had given the dragons and their new allies, the elves.

"My kynd are not perfect," Amona said in answer to Nix's question about a possible attack. "No kynd can be. The Jade matriarch, Eux, informed me that not all of the Jades came to the swearing in Red Meadow."

Vahly gripped the door handle. "What?"

Amona grimaced. "Eux believed all had come because of her command through the Call."

Nix's wings flicked in agitation as she tied her red hair into a knot on top of her head. "I made the announcement to all the Breakers at the ciderhouse. Euskal and Aitor spread the word. I don't think we missed anyone. I did a head count during the oath. They were all gathered up beside Miren."

Nix was right. Vahly had heard Euskal calling around when she'd been in Nix's rooms, helping her pack up. And Aitor had ignored the fact that his face had been all but ruined by a Jade and had gone off gladly to round up any Jade Breakers who didn't often come by Nix's. He'd returned with a full list of those attending the oath. On the day they all swore allegiance to Vahly, every Breaker who had ever crossed Nix's threshold—and many strangers as well—had stood near the bald-headed Miren.

Amona frowned at Arc, then looked back at Vahly, her eyes filled with concern. "Eux says there is a band of Breakers who keep far away from every other highbeast. They broke away years ago, and no one has seen them."

"They're probably dead." Vahly walked over to Arc, then tugged on his surcoat. "Every time I turn my back on you, you're trying to learn things. The reading will have to wait, my dear elf."

A sly grin slid over Arc's bow lips. "I don't mind being called *dear*."

Vahly's heart thudded inside her chest. She chuckled at herself and shook her head.

"Vahly." The matriarch's voice held the sharp edge of a

command, and Vahly found herself standing straight and listening intently. Their bonding was definitely still intact, and she was glad of it. It was almost as good as having Amona along on the journey. The security of knowing she had backup in the form of a matriarch was no small thing. Plus, the familiarity of her mother's voice eased her fears about what she might be headed into and how she might very well turn out to be too weak to fight the Sea Queen. "I don't think the Jade Breakers are dead. There are rams enough in the high mountains to feed a small group if they are smart about the way they hunt and manage the land."

Nix sniffed. "I would strongly prefer it if we didn't use the term Breakers for these miscreants."

Vahly grinned. "Like our Breakers aren't miscreants?"

Nix raised her chin haughtily. "My Breakers would never skip out on swearing allegiance to you, Earth Queen."

Smoke twisted from Amona's nostrils. "Only to me and to Eux, hm?"

Vahly held up a hand. "Let's remember we're all on the same side here. The past is the past. All right?" She dipped her head respectfully to Amona. "My matriarch?"

Amona let out a smoky breath, her gaze never leaving Nix. "You know, I put up with quite a bit from you and yours over the years. And you pulled my daughter into your schemes as well, even though she had no need for more gold."

"I didn't befriend her until she came to me, and by then, she was an adult, and she made her own decisions. With respect, Amona." Nix deigned to bow her head briefly.

Amona lips parted like she was about to say something, but then she closed her mouth.

"Time to go?" Vahly raised her eyebrows and forced her voice to sound cheerful. "Yes, I think it is time to go. Goodbye, Mother and Matriarch." She touched Amona's forearm.

The heat left Amona's gaze as she looked at Vahly. "I wish you safe travel. Be wary of the rogue Jades. They may not believe you are what we know you are, or they may simply kill without stopping to consider the consequences."

"Sounds about right," Vahly muttered.

"Call to me if you need aid," Amona said.

"Stars and Blackwater, Arc, come on," Vahly said, eyeing him as he replaced the scroll he'd been reading.

He joined her, and they started into the tunnel.

"Before these two light one another on fire," she whispered to Arc, jerking her head in the direction of the dragons.

Nix gave Amona one last nod, then walked behind them. "I think you and the elf are more likely to ignite than anyone else." She winked a large, yellow eye. One of her blue wings masked the side of her scaled, round-cheeked face.

Arc took the lead, allowing Nix and Vahly to walk side by side. The lantern's light flickered over his form, casting his powerfully shaped shadow across the tunnel's dry rock walls.

"Who would've guessed we'd be traveling with an elf?" Nix smirked.

"Not this lady," Vahly said.

Dark and narrower than any of the tunnels in the Lapis

dragon palace, the passageway twisted and turned under the earth like the belly of a petrified snake. Cool water dripped from the ceiling, gathering on Vahly's head and in the crook of her arms.

Buzzing and drumming through her feet, earth magic urged Vahly's legs to run, but she held back. This couldn't be a rushed trip. It was a good hike to the western mountains, and hurrying overmuch wouldn't do anything except wear her recently healed body out too soon.

In silence, they continued on as the tunnel began a slow ascent. Dim moonlight filtered in from the distance, showing spindly ferns and thick moss on the passageway's walls. A mouse squeaked and hurried past, making Nix grunt in disapproval.

"They could've tidied up a bit for us. You are a queen, after all," she muttered.

North of the main Lapis palace entrance, the tunnel opened into the Red Meadow. A crescent moon limned the flowers and the river, the sight forming a wish inside Vahly, a wish that they could stop here and enjoy the beauty instead of sneaking farther into the wilderness with no clue as to what they might find there.

Vahly's nerves sparked. What if she was leading Nix and Arc on a wild ferret chase? One that led to a death by either thirst or rogue Jades?

Built by her ancestors, a crumbling stone bridge reached to the far side of the river. Arc went across first, the endless night sky making him look small, and Nix followed, the edges and hollows of her wings collecting starlight like jewel dust.

The small stones of the bridge crunched beneath Vahly's

boots. "I'm seriously worried I'm dragging you two into an unending nightmare."

Nix snorted a laugh.

Arc turned, frowning. "I assure you, I'm fully awake. My nightmares involve a great deal more drama."

"More drama than following a leader who has no idea where she's going?" Vahly asked.

Arc glanced at her. "I know where we're going."

"I don't mean the trail. I mean, I'm not at all sure about this whole follow-my-gut thing."

Nix's wing brushed her arm. "What are our other choices? You don't have your full powers yet. We need to wake your magic completely or we have no chance against the Sea Queen."

"Indeed," Arc said quietly.

Nix spread her hands. "And anyway, I was bored."

Vahly rolled her eyes. This bravado was a mask. Nix just didn't want to stay around the ciderhouse where the imaginary ghosts of Dramour, Kemen, and Ibai haunted every corner. Nix needed time away. So did Vahly. Their loss was an avalanche waiting to start. If the details of whom they had lost crept into her immediate thoughts, if she indulged in any intimate memories, the whole mountain of grief would bury her. She simply could not think of Dramour's laugh, Kemen's conspiratorial nod, or Ibai's intense gaze as he mixed potions for healing.

Her eyes burned with hidden emotion as they came to the end of the bridge. She could almost hear her heart cracking, preparing for a life-altering fall. She cleared her throat of the thickness that had gathered there.

"But how long do we give this?" she asked.

Arc stopped to move his bow to his other shoulder while Nix and Vahly stood by the rippling water.

"What if we wander for an entire year?" Vahly asked. "An entire lifetime?"

Nix raised the scales above her eyes. "We'll be dead by the Sea Queen's hands long before any of that. Remember?"

Vahly crossed her arms. "Your bedside manner used to be much better."

Nix opened her mouth to say something, but the water churned at their feet.

Heart beating a tattoo on her chest, Vahly stepped back and hauled Nix with her.

Could the sea folk have somehow reached this fresh water?

A shimmering light like a blurred moon rose from the silver-tipped ripples. A voice tripped through the air, a singing, notes warbling and numbing Vahly's senses.

Shaking herself, Vahly stepped between the light and her friends.

"Be not afraid," the light said, the sound reminiscent of wind chimes.

Arc knelt beside Nix.

"What are you doing?" Vahly drew her sword as Nix growled at the being.

Head bent, Arc spoke quietly. "Earth Queen, Mistress of the Call Breakers, I present to you the Spirit of the River."

Vahly and Nix exchanged confused looks.

Vahly narrowed her eyes at the Spirit, trusting that Arc was not simply acting gullible. "A pleasure to meet you." She copied Arc and knelt in the sandy rocks beside the river's edge.

Nix took a knee as well. "Just how many secrets are you keeping, elf?" she hissed out of the corner of her mouth.

The Spirit rose higher in the water. Silver scales glittered around the edges of the Spirit's circular form. Vahly's breath caught at the beauty and strangeness.

"Don't fault the elven lord," the Spirit whispered, the words dropping slowly like honey from a summer comb. "Of the sparing few who know of me, I ask that they hold talk of my existence to themselves."

"With all respect," Vahly started, "why do you now present yourself to us?"

"The world needs you, Earth Queen, and I must do my part to aid you on your journey."

Vahly glanced at Nix, who shrugged. "Thank you. How exactly can you help?"

The Spirit dipped beneath the water for a moment, and a small wave lipped over the rocks to wet the toes of Vahly's boot. "I am no warrior, but I helped your kynd build this bridge, and I came to love them."

Images flickered to life at the far side of the bridge. Vahly stared in wonder as the ghostly shapes of humans accepted smoothed stones from a light that brought them to the surface—the Spirit was aiding them. There were at least a dozen humans, no, more than that. Males wearing hooded tunics digging a trench for drainage and laughing —the sound muffled and distant. Females with light hair like Vahly's stacking rocks and creating short walls. Youths shoving one another into the river playfully and bearing the lectures of their elders.

Vahly put a hand to her cheek and realized she'd been

crying. She wiped the tears away quickly, cheeks hot and her heart aching like a starving stomach.

The faint images faded, and Vahly battled the desire to run after them, to beg the Spirit to show them more.

Not noticing Vahly's secret longings, the Spirit spoke on. "When Astraea rose to power in the salt water realms, her aura tainted even my waters. Indeed, her foul ocean blacked my fresh currents during the flooding that took the last of your family, Earth Queen."

The Spirit spoke the Sea Queen's name like a curse. Vahly was with her on that sentiment.

Silver light surrounded a river rock deep under the current, then the Spirit seemed to lift it above the water. "Take this. When you need aid, press a kiss onto its surface, and I will do my best to rally the creatures of fresh water to your banner."

Vahly took the rock and grasped it tightly. The damp surface chilled her fingers, and the scent of algae and metal found her nose. What would it look like if this being rallied its creatures? Water snakes, spotted frogs, and salamanders racing over land to join Vahly at the coast?

A new thought sprang to mind, a child of the first.

What if Vahly could call up the creatures of the land? Was that already within her power? If so, she had no idea how to do it. Swallowing, she rose from her knee and stepped forward.

"Thank you, Spirit. May I ask how you summon your creatures? Is that something an Earth Queen should be able to do?"

The Spirit tipped to one side before righting itself. "I

don't have the knowledge of what an Earth Queen can or cannot do."

Vahly frowned, disappointment tugging at her like a deep fatigue. "Oh. Of course. Thank you for the gift."

Nodding once, the shimmering light lowered itself under the river's dancing surface. With a splash, it was gone, and Vahly was left with the uncomfortable knowledge that there was so much more to learn about the world she was meant to save. And yes, some discoveries might prove beneficial like this river being and this special rock, but other revelations would hold threats she hadn't prepared for, evils lurking unseen.

If she didn't figure out how to wake her magic in full soon, what she didn't know might kill her before the sea had its chance.

CHAPTER TWO

A rc stood and offered a hand to Nix, who accepted it as she muttered something about elves and their hidden scrolls.

Vahly remembered those scrolls, the ones stacked to the high ceiling in the now deceased King Mattin's room. Cassiopeia cared for them now. Would she share them with the dragons and with Vahly if they asked?

They left the river and continued across the Red Meadow, the moon bright overhead and the red hat flowers brushing Vahly's boots.

A short ridge of black rock rose like a wall. Arc hauled himself to the top. He had kept the Spirit of the River a secret. Was it because he didn't realize she could actually help them or because he wanted to keep some information to himself? Vahly's heart sagged.

No, Arc had proven himself trustworthy. He'd sworn himself to her, risked his life for her and for the dragons who raised her.

Vahly followed Arc up the boulder, her fingers finding holds almost as quickly as his. "I'm sure you have a good reason for not telling us about the Spirit. Care to share?"

Arc had stepped back and dusted himself clean as Vahly joined him on top of the boulder, but at her words, he paused and regarded her with mournful eyes. Nix flew over the stony surface, then landed beside them.

"In matters of magic and the magical beings in the world," Arc said, his gaze searching Vahly's face, "elves collect secrets like dragons hoard gold. There are countless things I know that you don't. I'm afraid I don't know what to share and what is a waste of your time. I had never seen the Spirit before this night, and I had no idea that it would aid you. You've probably never heard of several powerful spirits of this land. It's possible that the Spirit of the Mountain still lives in the remote areas where the dragons don't roam. Our island is large, truly more of a continent, and was only named an island by the Sea Queen who reigned five generations before Astraea. I don't know why we adopted the phrase. That's another story entirely, one I'm not privy to."

Vahly was staring. More powerful beings? Sugarrabota was a continent and not an island? It was only a matter of land measurement, so it didn't change anything, but it was a thought twist. The word "continent" made her feel less swamped by the vast ocean.

Clicking her tongue, Nix leaned toward Vahly's face, then Nix looked at Arc. "Slow down, elf. You're killing her brain. Now, what in Stones and Blackwater is the Mountain Spirit?"

Taking up their westerly route again, Vahly shook her

14

head. "Just spill everything you can. Even the strangest piece of information might help in ways you can't imagine."

Arc exhaled behind her. "All right. Well, the Mountain Spirit is a being ten or eleven feet in height, and it takes the appearance of tree bark—a type of burl. Legends say it has the strength of one hundred elves. I don't know anyone who has seen the Spirit. It is very skittish, if the scrolls are right. The wind won't speak of it."

Vahly looked over her shoulder to see him tilting his head to listen to the breeze. The wind tousled his ebony hair. He caught her gaze and smiled, and her heart turned over.

Nix batted a mosquito away. "So these spirits aren't descended from elves like the rest of us with two arms and two legs?"

The sound of Arc uncorking his water skin was loud in the night. "They are born of spirit. Of an energy beyond our ken."

"If the Mountain Spirit takes the appearance of tree bark," Vahly said, "it might be in tune with my earth magic."

A cluster of maple trees hid the moon but allowed the stars to sprinkle light over the dry, waving grasses.

"Do you wish to alter our course and head north to try to find it?" Arc asked.

Nix rummaged in her satchel and came out with a handful of finger-sized scorchpeppers. She offered one to Arc, who took it and chewed it neatly. Just the scent of them burned Vahly's nostrils.

The earth magic beating through Vahly's veins wouldn't

allow her to walk away from their mysterious quest into the western mountains. "No. I have to go west. My magic demands it."

"Is the sensation unpleasant?" Arc caught up and accepted another scorchpepper from Nix, who walked on the other side of Vahly.

Vahly shook her head. "It's just...insistent."

Talking around a small bite, Nix said, "What else do you know, Arcturus?"

"Haldus—do you remember him? The male with the wide-set frame who served as a guide within the Oaken Palace?"

Vahly nodded, recalling the elf who'd showed her to her rooms right before she'd accidentally barged into Arc's bath.

Arc didn't notice the sly grin tugging at Vahly's mouth. He continued, "Haldus once showed me a scroll about beings called *galtzagorri*. They were spirits who showed themselves to humans and sometimes did their bidding. They were like short, stout humans, but transparent. We believe they were only a story, one told to human younglings to keep them obedient."

The air dried Vahly's throat. Tomorrow was going to be a hot one. "Ah. So the humans told their sons and daughters 'Clean the dishes, and you might earn a galtzagorri who will do your chores for the rest of your life.'"

"Something like that," Arc said.

"What do you think will happen in the western mountains when we get there?" Vahly's cheeks warmed.

This was her quest, and she felt like a fool not knowing a single thing about it.

But it didn't seem to bother Arc. "I believe once we close in on the ruins of your kynd, your powers will increase. You may feel something...more."

Nix's stomach growled, and she ran a hand over her trim belly. "I could use something more."

Vahly gave Nix a withering look. They had eaten their way through nine courses with the Lapis before leaving. "The feast was only five hours ago."

Nix narrowed her eyes. "You have your inner longings. Allow me mine."

Pinching the bridge of her nose, Vahly sighed. "Fine. Once we get to that line of trees at the end of the Red Meadow, we'll do some hunting. How does that sound?"

Arc shushed them both, then crouched. "A stag," he whispered, the light and shadow of his magic curling around his fingers and temples. "Just there."

He nocked his bow with movements too quick to properly see.

Elves. Did they have to be so much faster and more graceful than everyone else?

"Nix, mask your scent," Arc whispered.

Nix's eyebrow raise was impressively high. "Mask your ego, elf."

Arc ignored her jab and raised his weapon. Sure enough, a deer skirted through the oaks, then stopped to turn its antlered head. Arc's arrow flew, and the simplebeast fell.

Soon, they had a small fire and some roasting meat.

The majority of the deer had gone to Nix, who had shifted into her battle dragon form to eat the meal raw.

Arc and Vahly sat on opposite sides of the fire.

"Do you know where your horse is now?" The venison's grease warmed Vahly's mouth, and the scent was familiar, comforting.

"Etor hasn't communicated with me since the day we left for the marshes."

"He isn't …"

"Dead? No." Arc began shoveling dirt onto the fire to cover their location. "I can feel that he still lives. He will return to me someday."

"How do you know?"

Arc shrugged. "I just do."

She glanced back at Nix. It was odd that Nix hadn't switched back into her human-like form to talk to them. She settled herself on the ground and spread one wing over her head to sleep. Vahly set her meal down, no longer hungry. Was Nix falling back into her grief? Vahly wanted to say something, to invite her over, but maybe Nix needed a moment.

Arc finished tamping the fire, then sat on a tree root, his legs set wide where they protruded from the slits in the sides of his surcoat. He unsheathed one of his throwing knives and began to sharpen the edge with a small whetstone. The grating sound quieted the evening birds and insects for a moment, but then the night's chorus rose again.

Vahly studied his face. He was still such a mystery to her despite all they'd been through. "Did you speak telepathically with the deer before you shot him?"

Arc glanced up, the moon catching in his eyes. "No. Royal-blooded elves, the only ones who have that ability, well, we are taught from a young age what is proper and what is not. Using telepathy to hunt is bent magic. Wrong. I would never do it."

"I'm sorry. I didn't intend to offend you."

"You did not know. No offense taken."

"Can you hear the birds' thoughts right now?" In the branches above, dark spots flitted through the moon shadows.

Arc shook his head. "Not unless I focus on them and they are willing."

"They have to be willing? They can think like that? So self-aware?"

"Some can. I don't attempt to read the minds of simplebeasts unless it seems beneficial and proper to both parties."

"If I didn't know you fully plan to do some wild experiment with dragonfire and Stones knows what else just to gain a unique power no one has yet to wield, I'd think you were a real goody-goody."

Arc laughed, his head falling back. "I don't do it to keep the power for myself. It would be for all kynds."

She held up a hand. "No, don't ruin it, elf. If you're too nice, you won't be any fun at all on this quest."

A wicked smile crossed Arc's features, crinkling his eyes at the corners.

But then his face fell.

He stood in a blink and threw both of his knives into the darkness behind Vahly.

A yowling erupted, loud enough to have Nix awake and breathing smoke, ready to fight.

Vahly shot to her feet, heart in her mouth. She turned to see a bear on the ground, its eyes vacant. One of Arc's knives stuck out from his chest and the other from his eye. She stared, frozen. She hadn't even drawn her sword. The bear was so close. Those animals were quick. It could have killed her in less than a minute if Arc hadn't been paying attention. Stones and Blackwater, she had to be better about journeying in the wilds like this. She'd grown far too complacent spending time with a bevy of dragons.

Arc looked nothing like a goody-goody now, not with that deadly focus in his eyes and the tense muscles of his chest rising and falling. Purple and pale yellow magic twirled around his temples and fingertips. At that moment, he was every inch the very dangerous, very skilled, royal elven warrior.

Nix blew a few sparks of dragonfire and shook her great head. In a circle of bright fire, she transformed. "I'm not overly fond of the wilderness aspect of being your loyal warrior, Vahly." She retrieved her clothing and dressed, mumbling to herself. "Bears. Hunger. I truly wonder why those rogue Jades Amona told us about chose to live this way, away from civilization. It's deplorable." When she was fully clothed—and had every one of her rings back on her fingers—she sat beside Vahly.

Arc hurried to the bear and whispered a few words over the dead beast. "I almost did not notice him. The flowers' scent here is strong and covered the bear's odor. He nearly dragged those lethal claws across your back."

Vahly's hands shook. "Thank you, Arc. I owe you one."

"I am fairly certain that is not how fealty works."

With enviable strength, he dragged the bear into a brushy area where the scavengers could do their work. Bears tasted foul, and their meat was stringy, so the kill was of no help to the always hungry Nix.

"Now," Arc said, "why don't we get some sleep before moving onward?"

Agreeing, Vahly set her satchel on the ground and tried to get comfortable. Nix lay down on her left, and Arc settled himself on her right.

Heat crept into her face. They were protecting her with their very bodies. She wasn't worthy. Not yet. "You two are worse than Amona."

"Deal with it," Nix whispered.

Arc faced the starry sky. In the moonlight, his skin was like a type of steel she'd never seen, more golden than silvery, of course, but strong and lined here and there from battle. "I won't sleep, Earth Queen." His lips moved quickly, and her fingers longed to touch them, to feel their velvet softness, to see how fierce they could be in a kiss. "I don't need the rest," he said. "But I'll be here. Just say the word, and I will do as you wish."

She wanted to thank him, but she was shy suddenly, awkward about being the center of all this attention. "Great. I hope you don't mind snoring, because I can really saw some logs, my friend."

A quiet laugh came from Nix and Arc both.

The conversation, the bear—all of it helped them avoid talking about their ongoing grief. Vahly was just fine with that for now.

A brief thought pinched her mind. Where were those enemy dragons? Nearby?

She fought sleep as long as she could, listening for the crack of branches or the rumble of dragon voices. Finally, fatigue stole her motivation and wrapped her in slumber.

CHAPTER THREE

The familiar flora and fauna of the Red Meadow and its forested border—red deer, oaks, beech, berry bushes, and rabbits—gave way to ancient olive trees with pale and twisted trunks, low scrub, sandy ground, and the long-tailed birds that sped along the ground instead of flying.

Smooth rock rose higher and higher as they made their way into the western mountains, the sun rising bright and piercing over their heads.

The magic inside Vahly tugged hard and she sucked a breath in surprise.

It felt like a hook had been threaded through her ribcage, right below her heart, and something invisible had yanked the barb to grab her attention. The feeling, though incredibly odd, didn't hurt. She only felt ...incomplete.

"We must be getting closer," she said, a hand on her chest.

Arc and Nix nodded and gave her twin looks of sympathy as she started walking again.

What did her magic yearn for?

She wished they could've questioned Mattin before fighting and being forced to kill him. He'd been the oldest of the elves still living and had known enough about human power rituals to nearly thwart Vahly before she'd truly had time to begin this journey to become the Earth Queen.

All they knew now was that Vahly had more to do before her power woke in full. At least, that was the most optimistic viewpoint, and the one Vahly was betting on.

The three of them worked their way along what had once been a road, a path wide enough for two wagons to pass side by side. The only sign left that it had been a thoroughfare was the flattened earth where only a few weedy plants managed to thrive. Ancient olive trees grew toward the clear sky. The sun climbed in time with Vahly, Arc, and Nix, its white heat unusually powerful for a day this late in the summer. It was very nearly autumn.

Sweat trickled down the back of Vahly's neck, and the top of her head was on fire. She pulled her skin of water from her satchel and finished the last of the lukewarm liquid.

"Can we search for a spring?" she asked.

Nix sniffed the air. She gestured toward two promising-looking boulders that came together to form a dark recess. "There might be water in that small cave."

Arc cocked his head, listening to something the rest of them couldn't hear. "Possibly."

The opening in the mountain swallowed them. The air didn't smell damp to Vahly. She hoped Nix's nose was working better than her own because they wouldn't get far without more water. The last time Vahly had been in this region, traveling with Amona, the awful Lord Maur, and a small group of warriors, the land hadn't been nearly as dry. Yes, it'd always been far less lush than the Lapis territory, but the rising seas had definitely affected this area in a foul manner. Something about the encroaching spelled salt water drew the life right out of the earth.

Vahly blew out a heavy breath, wishing with everything she had that her magic wasn't so picky about when it was going to show up. Time was not something they had to waste.

Nix's yellow eyes flashed in the dim light as she knelt to touch the cave floor. "Dry." Sighing, she removed her own water skin and shook it, trying to get the last drop.

Arc bent to reach into a crevice between a rock with a glassy surface and a boulder that had broken from the larger expanse above their heads.

The tug in Vahly's ribs increased in intensity.

She put a hand over her heart, feeling a little lightheaded. She almost said *I'm meant to be here,* but she managed to hold her tongue despite the powerful urge to declare her feelings. The whole situation was bizarre, and she felt foolish talking overmuch about it. But there was no doubt in her. Her earth magic was insistent on her exploring this cave.

But why?

"There is water below," Arc said.

Was that the sole reason? Well, they did need water if they were going to continue to follow Vahly's gut. She approved of how practical her magic seemed to be.

"I'll get down there." Her sword and bow clanked

against a rock as she removed them. She had to be the one to go, because Arc and Nix were too big to squeeze into that space.

"You're certain you'll be able to climb out again?" Nix eyed the space, the corners of her mouth tipping down as if she wanted nothing to do with it.

"Sure. I only ate one rasher of bacon as opposed to my normal two yesterday," Vahly said wryly. "But if you could work up one of those light orbs of yours, Arcturus, that would be very helpful."

"Of course." As Arc spun a glowing sphere from the air, the sound of his magic rose, a distant howl like the wind on a stormy night. Hair slightly mussed from the gust of wind that accompanied his creation, he handed the orb to Vahly.

The light dimmed as she touched it, but the miniature suns floating about inside the transparent sphere still managed to illuminate the space as well as a small torch.

"How long will this work for me?" she asked.

"I don't know, actually. I've never handed one off to a human."

Nix looked over the ground. "I can torch a branch for you if we find one." She picked up a sad little stick, then dropped it. "Nah. There's nothing here that'll work. Stick with the magic of elf balls."

Vahly snickered as she lowered herself into the crevice, but she heard Arc's reply to Nix.

"I'm so glad you are finally beginning to appreciate the prowess of my kynd," he teased Nix, his voice echoing off the walls as Vahly climbed down.

Vahly maneuvered into the crevice, then underneath a low shelf of rock. "Nix has been admiring your prowess since we left," she called up to them. "And by prowess, I mean your arse."

The space Vahly wiggled into quickly widened into a room with damp, heavy air and a constant drip from an unseen source. The pull in her drummed in rhythm with her pulse as earth magic sang through her boots and into her feet. She climbed over a tumble of smaller stones, scattering a few hand-sized cave spiders.

A shudder rocked her. She'd always hated the little beasties.

"Why did it have to be spiders?" she muttered, forcing herself onward.

Arc's orb glinted, weakly illuminating the end of the space. Vahly knelt and ran a hand along the dark rocks at her feet, feeling for a spring. All was dry, so she pushed her fear of more arachnid beasties to the back of her mind and stretched to reach farther down.

Finally, moisture wetted her skin. Using thumb and finger, she tried to dislodge one of the stones in hopes that disturbing the spot would allow the water to flow freely enough to fill her water skin.

Idly, she wondered if she could use her earth magic to move the rocks. Her power was weak at best and, of course, tied to her own energy levels. Right now, she was tired and parched. She managed to work another rock away from the water source, deciding to hold off on using magic to save it for instances in which nothing else would do the job. Best not to risk it at the bottom of a cave, in any case.

The water bubbled over the back of her hand, cold and refreshing. If she could get a hold on one final stone—an incredibly smooth and oddly shaped one—perhaps the spring would be fully accessible. She pushed the strange rock, trying to shift it. The thing rolled back, slid over her hand completely, then knocked along the ground, rolling to a stop out of sight. It wasn't nearly as heavy as it should've been.

She scrambled to where it might have halted, and sure enough, an opening to a spring appeared. Water flowed at a steady enough pace to fill her water skin. Well, it would once she moved the rolled stone.

Wait. It wasn't a stone.

She set the light orb down, then lifted the stone that wasn't a stone.

Purple flecks colored the seamless surface. Vahly tapped it.

Something inside scratched back.

She nearly dropped it, her own heart hammering along with the earth's ever-present heartbeat. It was an egg. And her tingling fingers and the sound drumming in her ears made it very clear this was no normal egg.

Whatever lived in this shell belonged to her, and, equally, she belonged to it.

Forgetting the water and her parched throat entirely, she cradled the egg, and then maneuvered her way back to the crevice to the upper level. She looked up, her hand steady on the egg, and an ache spread through her chest—a feeling similar to being on the brink of crying.

Arc's eyebrows rose as he peered down. Nix leaned over too, her pupils dilating in that dragon way beside a second light orb Arc must've created.

"Water," Nix said slowly. "We needed water." She glanced at Arc. "I think our friend here must have bumped her skull. She's forgotten the goal completely. We can get eggs from the trees, darling Vahly."

But the fire in Vahly's returning look must've shown them exactly how important this egg somehow was.

They immediately set to work helping her bring the egg carefully up to their level.

Once Arc had secured the egg, Vahly filled all three of their water skins at the mouth of the spring—the place the egg had revealed to them. Because that was exactly the truth of it. The egg had brought her to the place where she and her cohorts could find proper water flow. Every beat of the earth inside Vahly's Blackwater blessed blood sang the truth of it.

A word whispered through her mind. *Familiar.*

Climbing back out of the crevice to join Nix and Arc, Vahly did her best to remain calm. What did that word mean? How was it related to a large egg? Was this the end of her quest? Had she found the reason her magic had been pushing her into the western mountains? So many questions. Her mind burned for the answers.

Arc nestled the egg inside Vahly's satchel, which sat beside her bow and sword belt. She held her breath as he adjusted it, but he was careful, keeping the buckle on the flap from clipping the delicate exterior.

The egg held her attention in full as a buzz ran through Vahly's chest. She had found a friend, solid and trustworthy. But how did she know this? None of it made any sense. This unborn creature was her confidante?

Nix's mouth lifted, and she ran a gentle, taloned hand over the shell, looking to Vahly as she approached. "What do you think is hiding in there?" Nix asked.

Vahly shrugged, wishing she had more answers than questions. "I don't know."

Arc sat and crossed his legs, appearing far too calm. They needed to rush outside with the egg and do some kind of celebratory dance or something to show the world how excited she was about this find.

"I know what it is," Arc said quietly, frowning.

A weight settled on Vahly. He didn't seem pleased. "Don't hold back on your elvish wisdom now." Vahly knelt beside him.

"It's a gryphon egg," he said.

Disbelief slid through the cave. There hadn't been a gryphon spotted as long as Vahly had been alive. And from the scrolls she'd read looking for clues to her power ritual, they'd been extinct for at least a century.

Nix fell back, mouth open. "This is even more shocking than the idea that the elves continued to flourish for so long without the rest of us knowing a thing about it."

"Are you sure?" Vahly asked Arc, touching the egg and feeling the echoing scratch against the underside of the surface.

Arc nodded. "Those plum-hued spots only show up on a gryphon egg. I too had thought they'd passed from this world."

Vahly stood, then sat again, unable to be still. She gripped Arc's bare forearm, feeling the warmth and strength of his elven flesh and bone. "I can feel the creature inside." She touched her heart, where the tugging sensation was strongest. "When do you think it will hatch?"

Arc's head dropped. He looked up at Vahly through a thick lock of his raven hair. "It will not hatch."

Vahly's heart seized, and she jumped to her feet, bumping her head on the cave's sharp ceiling. Rubbing the pain away, she peppered Arc with questions. "But why? How do you know? Did elves study gryphons? You can't possibly know for certain."

Nix took a long drink from her water skin, then handed it to Vahly. "Drink. If you die of thirst, none of this will matter."

Vahly did as Nix suggested, taking a quick sip. Her body wanted more, but her mind didn't have room for worrying about that.

Arc stood, arms crossed and eyes sad. "They died off due to a general failure to hatch. We have records of it in our scrolls. The gryphons once thrived in the Red Meadow and the mountains here and to the north. But after the first of the major wars between elves, humans, and dragons, the new eggs never managed to hatch. No one knows exactly why, but the accepted reason is the gryphons didn't have enough prey. The smaller animals were driven out of the area by dragonfire spreading through the underbrush, and the hungry gryphon adults bore offspring that died in the shell."

Vahly blinked, wishing Arc were more often wrong in his assumptions. Her limbs filled with sand, and the ground suddenly looked inviting for a long sleep and a good cry.

Nix eyed Arc like she might consider him for her next meal. "Elves. You're always blaming it on the dragons. Your kynd started that first war, Arcturus, if I remember the tales correctly."

Arc's nostrils flared. "Only because you had infringed on our hunting grounds."

Vahly held up her hands. "Peace, you two. I thought you'd grown fond of one another. Where did the fondness run off to, hm?"

"He's fine," Nix muttered. "Lucky he's so pretty."

Arc looked down, amusement showing on his full lips.

Vahly tucked the egg farther into her satchel and lowered the flap over the shell. Heavy and sluggish, she pulled her bow over her back, then buckled her sword belt around her waist.

Arc and Nix drank more from their water skins as they argued.

Vahly's thoughts clung to the egg. Why was she meant to find a gryphon egg? Especially if it wouldn't hatch? Was her magic faulty? Perhaps the earth's drumming and that tug near her heart were only aftereffects of the fever she'd suffered. This couldn't be the Source's plan. An egg? What was the point?

Daylight drifted through the break in the rocks, and Vahly started toward it while Arc and Nix talked quietly behind her.

Before leaving the cave, Vahly set a hand against her satchel. Beneath the fabric, the egg's shape curved against her palm. "What is the deal with you, egg?" she whispered. "I hate to drag your unborn tail into this mess of a life I've made here. Wouldn't you rather stay in this cave? You might have a better chance of hatching in this safe place."

Perhaps it was her imagination, but Vahly felt a hard thump against her palm. "The creature inside just bumped me again. It's alive. I know it. I think it'll hatch. He is strong."

Arc's voice rose. "He?"

The knowledge swelled over Vahly's mind, sure as the rising sun. "The gryphon is male. I don't know how I know that. But I do." She patted the egg and walked into the sun.

"Maybe this is tied to your earth magic too," Nix said.

They walked in silence, all of them puzzling furiously.

CHAPTER FOUR

Queen Astraea glided through the ocean, grinning at the power that sang through her blood. Soon, Ryton would return. He'd be triumphant, and there would be no cause to worry about the flood failing. All would be well. She wished he'd already reported back, but perhaps he was enjoying himself. Taking time to kill the blooming Earth Queen with style.

Astraea quite liked that idea.

How would he do it exactly? Driving water into her lungs? Spearing her through, limb by limb, to watch her slowly die?

The ocean would devour the human's blood like it did every other creature's. This Earth Queen would die, one way or another, as all would die. This one would perish at Queen Astraea's command.

Schools of silvery longfish broke apart, then fled the queen's sudden approach, their strategy of clustering together to appear larger forgotten entirely.

The wide-open water went on for miles upon miles. Light drifted from the surface and turned the shallow levels of the water a pale green. Astraea stretched her arms wide, kicking her feet. The expanse of her world was marvelous. And it was all under her control. No one else's. She was the most powerful creature. None could force her to submit. Never again would she be the fearful creature of her youth, suffering her mother and father's slaps and insults, their fingers tight in her hair, the bubbles from their mouths hot and stinking on her cheek.

Never again.

A shark five times Astraea's size darted from the shadows of a sunken human ship.

The queen's heart tripped in reaction, but just as quickly, her pulse normalized. This simplebeast was no match for her.

"Take me into your maw if you think you can!" Her magic vibrated around her words like plucked strings.

The ocean tasted of death and blood. This shark had killed recently.

Plunging toward her at a breakneck speed, the shark opened its mouth to show rows of pointed teeth.

The poor beast thought it could end her.

She cackled, bubbles rising from her coral-red lips. A spell came to her mind, as magic often did, and she raised her arms, speaking the ancient words of power. Words that were as old as the world itself. The sounds were hollow, then snapping. Long, then howling. They were like beasts themselves, set loose to do her bidding.

A floral taste touched the queen's mouth, her magic's

flavor, and a current whirled to life. As the water rushed away from her, it tried to tangle her tightly knotted blue-green hair. She shifted, and the blast of spelled salt water gushed toward the black-finned shark.

The spell whipped the creature from its path, currents blasting the knife-edge tail and collapsing one entire side of the great body. His head seemed distorted, wrenched down in pain, jaws slack.

Astraea did not stop there.

"You should've had the good sense to bow to your queen."

She poured more of her energy into the spellwork and the whirling currents of white-green. Water drove into the shark's open mouth. The creature jerked hard, tail slicing the eddies in an instinct to survive, to flee this horror he'd dared to face.

The queen fisted her free hand as her spellwork pummeled the shark toward the sea floor. Her cheeks lifted into a vicious grin and a glint sparked from her eyes as the creature twitched, then grew still.

Without another look, Astraea swam away from her victim. A sense of triumph colored the world in bright shades of blue, green, and gold. This was exactly the way the world was meant to be. With Astraea as the supreme power.

Only in this particular version of life could the queen smile, dance, and swim proudly. If even one beast, simple or high, tread upon her place as ultimate ruler, she'd lose it all.

Her confidence. Her strategic mind. Her magic.

If anyone or anything caused her to submit, her past

would crawl out of the darkness and bury her. If she failed to destroy any barrier, any usurper, she would hate herself again. She would see, in her mind's eye, that little one she had been so long ago.

A sad shadow in a house of fists and degradation.

Her stomach turned at the broken memory. Fermented sea violets. Their clinging stink. The way those hands— hands that should have cared for her, loved her—shoved the intoxicating violets down her young throat. The laughter that scratched against the gray coral walls and pierced her eardrums as well as any bone needle.

Astraea's legs beat against the water, shaking the memory away. She swam hard and forced a smile. No one would ever submit her to their will. Ever again.

She would die first.

BEYOND A WALL OF WAVING SEAGRASS, THE CITY OF WODE'S Current appeared. Tailors with their shops of pale blue stone lined the main street, which led into a square of sandstone guild houses.

The sea folk bowed as Astraea passed, snippets of their whispered words tickling her ears. They knew she was headed to a music concert at the house of the wealthiest family in the sea, the size of their fortune second only to her own. Pearce controlled the pearl trade alongside his quiet wife, Acantha. At events, Astraea had seen her acting docile and shy, only to suddenly snap into a rage at surrounding young ones. Most likely, she treated their daughter in such a way.

Pearce claimed their daughter Larisa had a golden voice.

Singing, music, painting—the arts deserved top billing in the world, just behind war and power. The arts deserved wholehearted respect. If this pearl merchant's daughter was worth the praise folk were piling on her, Astraea would gladly invite her to court to escape her parents and play for the upcoming battle feast.

And what a celebration it would be.

Soon, Astraea would flood the Lapis territory. Many sea warriors would be slain. She knew that well. Such risks deserved reward, so before the flooding commenced, Astraea would welcome her warriors to a grand spread of the ocean's finest offerings, steamed and seasoned by the castle chefs. There would be countless pleasures at their fingertips. It was only right to shower those willing to give up their lives with praise, food, and the best of the arts before the big day.

If only Ryton would hurry. He should've been back already. No human could match him in the water.

Surely.

True, this was an Earth Queen he was set on killing, but still. The Earth Queen hadn't struck out at the sea yet, so she could not be as powerful as Astraea had first feared. So what was taking Ryton so long?

Two rows of blooming firestalks led Astraea to an arched doorway. Between the open doors, Pearce and Acantha stood with twin smiles of welcome.

Astraea swept past them and into their entryway. The marble floors were cool on her bare feet as she walked, head high, the couple scurrying to catch up.

Pearce rambled on and on about improvements made to

the house and how pleased they were to have the queen as a guest.

"Yes, yes." Astraea's patience thinned. "The audition will be in this room?" She pointed to a set of bright red doors in the center of the home, the usual spot for gatherings in sea folk houses.

Acantha opened the door. "Yes, please go in. The servants will provide you with refreshment."

Three uniformed servants scattered like startled needlefish as Astraea found a settee and made herself comfortable.

"That is not necessary," Astraea said. "Let us hear your daughter. Where is she? I don't have time to linger overlong."

A thin female with a long face entered the room from a passageway in the back corner. She bowed gracefully to Astraea. So this was Larisa. Her hair was braided neatly on top of her head, pearls threaded so thickly that the room's luminescent nautili glittered off her as if she herself also glowed.

Astraea smiled genuinely at Larisa, pleased with her demeanor and appearance.

"Please begin when you are ready," Astraea said in a softer tone that she rarely used. So often, folk disappointed her in the ugly way they spoke or acted. Larisa had more grace than her parents had ever possessed.

"This is our sweet angelfish." Pearce lifted his chin and held out a hand as if he were presenting a particularly profitable shipment to a prospective buyer. "She is quite—"

Astraea's gaze cut him off. "She can speak for herself. Can't you, lovely one?"

Larisa bowed again, her fins rippling gently in the current. "Yes, my queen. Thank you for coming to hear me. I hope I will please you."

The settee was soft on Astraea's back. "I'm sure you will."

Larisa glanced at her parents, then, with their nod of approval, she opened her mouth and sang. Notes swam through the silver bubbles coming from her lips. The sound waves rippled to Astraea's ears. Low and mellow, high and sweet, the notes tripped and stretched.

Astraea's heart surged. Only truly astounding music could move her, and here it was, in the flesh. Astraea's eyes burned as she stood, wanting to get closer, to hear her more clearly, to better take in every line of undulating sound.

A servant near the doors knocked an elbow into the wall, and Larisa's voice caught and stumbled. She corrected the mistake quite quickly. The hitch resulted from youth and inexperience. That was all. She would grow stronger with time.

At the conclusion of the piece, Larisa's parents rushed over to apologize to Astraea for the slight mistake.

"Please forgive her, my queen," Pearce said.

"You deserve better, Queen Astraea," Acantha said. She turned and slapped Larisa across the face. Blood leaked into the water and hung around Larisa's head like a crown.

Astraea's childhood came roaring back. Her family had replaced the pearl merchant, the wife, and Larisa. She saw her mother's hand striking and felt her own blood sliding away. Fear chilled her veins and tried to tell Astraea she would never have power over her own life. Not with the

BAND OF BREAKERS

Touched mark. Not with her parents using her status like pieces on a chess board.

Fury boiled around Astraea's heart.

On the day she'd cut down her beastly parents, she'd vowed none would have power over her. And in Larisa's face, Astraea saw her own.

She sped to Larisa's side, touched the split lip, and said a spell to heal it.

Then Astraea faced Acantha. "How dare you lay your filthy hands on this jewel."

Memories of her own parents' cruel hands writhed inside her mind.

Blocking out Acantha's apologies, Astraea called up a spell, and the water began to churn. Currents whirled faster than even she could see. Using her coral spear, she threw the spelled water, and Acantha fell back. Pearce tried and failed to catch his wife as the magical current twisted her body to smash against the wall.

A garish coral sculpture of a dolphin detached from its mount, the pathetic excuse for artwork crashing into Acantha's head. Blood poured from the wound as she moaned, and Pearce shouted for his servants. Acantha jerked, then went limp, her body floating in the ruby water. The female was dead.

Larisa started toward her horrible mother, but Astraea stayed the girl with a hand. "You don't owe that monster a thing, darling. Come with me."

With Pearce stammering pleas, apologies, and calls to his healer, Astraea swam from the house. Larisa followed quietly in her wake.

"Never let lesser beings diminish you," Astraea said as

they swam through town, nodding to the bowing passersby. "You have a power in that voice of yours, and you must use it to rule your own little kingdom. A kingdom I'll create for you at court." Astraea smiled. It would be pleasant to have a protégé of sorts.

"But you killed her." Larisa's lip trembled. "That was... she was my mother."

Astraea paused to press a finger to Larisa's shaking mouth. "Do not spare another thought for her. Or for your father. You are made for greater things. Acantha would've killed you if I'd have let her continue. Not today. But soon. I know how these things happen. Trust me. I'm your true patron and supporter."

Just then, Astraea remembered that Grystark had asked to speak to her. He'd argue about the way she'd sent Ryton to slay the Earth Queen. He'd be worried for his old friend. Such weakness of spirit! Such vanity to disagree with one's queen! She grimaced, her stomach turning as she imagined the spark of judgment in his old eyes. Smoothing her features, she smiled at Larisa.

"You don't need those beastly parents, and I won't allow you to demean yourself by mourning their loss. Don't worry, little fish. I'll teach you everything you need to know. Your lessons will begin today. I will show you how to bring a soul to heel."

CHAPTER FIVE

Vahly walked beside Arc, while Nix went on a step or so ahead, stopping now and then to pick an unusual plant and taste it carefully with the tip of her blue tongue. Nix winced at a white stalk of green flowers that looked like small hands, but when she sampled a tall, orange weed with tiny branches that waved in the warm breeze, her eyebrows lifted, and she ate the entire plant.

The egg and the problem of its existence pressed against Vahly's every thought, shoving all other concerns to the very back of her mind. "Why would less prey mean fewer eggs hatched?" she asked Arc.

He moved the strap of his large bag, smoothing a wrinkle from the material of his surcoat, along the muscles of his chest. "The young inside weren't strong enough to live, to break through the shell when the time came to emerge."

"Could we break the shell open ourselves?"

"I think that would be fatal to the creature." He eyed her

satchel. "Gryphons were originally very hardy simplebeasts. Some stories claimed they even had a form of magic themselves."

Nix glanced at them over her shoulder, her wings fluttering. "What form? Air? Fire? I assume it must be one of those due to its ability to fly." The lapis-studded clips in her red hair reflected the sun. Dramour had bought the clips for her with his winnings last summer.

"That's a good question," Arc said. "I don't know."

The egg's presence pulled at Vahly's heart, and she touched the satchel just to feel its shape again. "I have a bond with it. It's ridiculous, but I do. I have to help him hatch."

"What's that plant you are devouring, Nix?" Concern tightened the syllables of Arc's words.

Nix waved a stalk she'd plucked to bring along. "Tastes like bacon."

"A plant that tastes of meat? Intriguing. May I try some?" Arc took a piece from Nix and bit down on the bright orange branches. They seemed to be softer than most weeds. "I hope this doesn't kill me."

Vahly's stomach growled fiercely. "Does it taste like hog?"

"It does indeed," Arc said. "And if I'm not mistaken, it is helping me see more clearly. Did you notice that as well, Nix? Odd. And worrisome. I've never come across such a plant."

Nix dropped back. "Yes. I can see the tops of the Bihotzetik ruins. That's a cathedral's spire in the midst of the waves, isn't it?"

Arc nodded.

"Well, give me some of that magical bacon." Vahly took a piece from Nix's clawed hand, then chewed it quickly.

The distant water slowly grew clearer. Foam-tipped waves framed the glassy black stone spires of the fallen human city.

Bihotzetik. *From the heart.*

Vahly's heart surged. This was the last powerful hold of earth kynd.

The earth's drumming pounded through her bones, and a feeling like static electricity ran up her legs before spreading into her chest, arms, and up the back of her neck. A tingling sensation poured down her scalp, then the scent of sun-warmed earth filled her nose.

She took a long breath, feeling fully alive and fully herself. The magic was speaking to her, showing her that she had to get into that ruined city.

"Vahly?" Arc tilted his head and smiled tentatively. He and Nix had both turned to stare. "You look ..." His gaze traveled over her face as if he could find the descriptive word he wanted written in her features.

"My magic. It's speaking to me. Like it did after I washed in the Blackwater and when I found the egg."

Nix glanced at the sunken city, then she looked at Vahly again. Her blue scales glittered in the sun. "And it has to do with the city."

The tallest of the five spires was indeed the Bihotzetik cathedral. It'd been a place of worship for over two millennia before the sea kynd had lifted the ocean and flooded the entire metropolis, killing every inhabitant. Only those humans in the mountains where Vahly, Nix, and Arc now stood had lived through the attack. The survivors had

45

been forced to relocate to the Lost Valley, where Vahly had been born.

Holding a hand up to block the sun and squinting hard enough to give her a headache, Vahly tried to make out the cathedral spire's shape—three curved oak leaves that came to a point at the very top.

The scrolls she'd found on human history explained the cathedral's tie to earth magic and the sacred oak. Vahly shook her head. Every one of her kynd, from child to elder, had known all the ins and outs of earth magic. She knew less than any in history.

But at least the magic was speaking to her. That was something.

"I have to go there. To the city."

"We're still going with that wild idea, are we?" Nix's voice strained. "To get as close to the ruins as we can?" She swallowed, her lips turned down in a look that some would think was disgust. It was actually fear.

And Vahly was about to make it worse. She breathed out slowly. "I'm not going close. I'm going *in*."

Arc threw the remainder of his orange plant to the ground.

Nix snatched it up. "What are you doing?"

"If this plant has anything to do with Vahly wanting to risk venturing into the sea kynd's realm, I want no part of it." He faced Vahly. "You're the hope of the world. This is impossible. Recklessness could very well be an effect of this food source."

"It's not the plant," Vahly said. "My magic tells me I have to go there. And reckless is pretty much my middle name, so you'd best get used to this type of thing."

Nix pointed to a game trail heading parallel to the coastline, its faint line perpendicular to the path they were currently following. "Let's head that way. We can scope out the ocean and maybe check through some ruins."

"You're ignoring me," Vahly said. "Listen. You know how your fire magic feels when the lightning rises for you in the clouds and your belly burns with power?"

Nix raised her face to the sky, a wistful expression painting her beautiful features. She sighed, smoke drifting from her nostrils, then met Vahly's gaze with intense eyes. She remained silent and staring. Vahly did not flinch.

Nix rolled her eyes. "Fine. If you're that sure. To the ocean we go, Earth Queen."

Vahly looked to Arc, waiting for him to agree. What if he refused to help? Would the heart promise he made to her kill him? Her stomach twisted and her skin itched. She didn't want her two closest advisors, her dearest friends, to be forced to agree with her.

Arc rubbed his hands roughly through his jet-black hair. "As you wish, my queen. But we will have to be quick."

A weight off her shoulders, Vahly walked on. They followed. "Yes. Like spies. Nix trained me to be quick."

"And you know how to swim?" Arc asked. "I have had plenty of chances to swim in freshwater in my homeland, but you—"

"I swam in the Silver River every summer day of my childhood," Vahly said. "No worry on that end of things."

"Accessing the ruins won't be the same. Those currents are strong enough to drag you out to sea."

A shiver gripped Vahly and shook her hard.

Nix nodded to Arc. "He's right. I'm guessing you'll

want to do more than glance at the top of the cathedral and the guild house. You'll need to dive deep and be under for a long time, Vahly."

She hadn't thought that through, but Nix was correct. Vahly tapped the hilt of her sword, thinking. "Nix, you can be our land watch, all right?"

"Definitely."

"And Arc, you can use your air magic telepathy to talk to Nix as needed?"

"Not a problem."

"But if we can't stay under long," Vahly said, "I can't imagine us accomplishing much."

Arc lifted his hands, eyes wide. "Ah! I know."

"I'm all ears," Vahly said.

"Was that an elf joke?" Arc raised a handsome eyebrow and wiggled one pointed ear.

Nix bumped his hip with hers and gave him a flirty grin. "Spill your idea, Master Alchemist."

"I can use air magic to breathe underwater." He spread a hand over his mouth to demonstrate. "Perhaps I can use the same power on you."

Vahly shrugged as she stepped over a hill of busy ants beside a vine of dark purple flowers, flora never seen in Lapis territory. "I'm up for trying that."

A square structure of pitted walls rose above the game trail. The humans had carved three small windows in the shape of oak leaves at the top of each wall. It looked like a watchtower, a spot that could oversee happenings on the surrounding high elevations as well as any disturbances at sea. As they passed the open doorway, Vahly glanced inside.

Sunlight streamed through the high windows and along what used to be a set of wooden stairs. Now, the wood showed only a railing and part of the landing at the top where the watchman would've stood. On the ground, vines grew from the remnants of a mosaic floor. Brown, black, and green tiles formed half of a human face. The sight stopped Vahly in her tracks. Her fingers latched onto the doorframe, her throat tightening. The subject of the mosaic had very blue eyes, not unlike her own. Near the image's chin, a pile of dirt and a small sapling sprouted from something that could have been stones.

It was a skeleton. Ice ran down Vahly's spine.

Arc and Nix silently followed her inside the tower, their quiet like a spell cast to freeze time.

Vahly held tight to the strap of her satchel, feeling the comforting weight of the egg. She crouched beside the skull. Why had this human died here? After all, they were above the sea. Shifting the plants crawling from the bones, she found the hilt of a dagger right where the heart would've been. Finger bones lay in small piles under the ribcage, perhaps where they had fallen from their grip on the hilt. The human had done this with her own hands. Chilled to the core, Vahly could almost feel the blade cutting through her own flesh.

Swallowing, she looked at Arc and Nix. They regarded her with solemn expressions. "This human saw the disaster. And killed herself."

Arc pressed a hand against the skeleton's femur and whispered something.

Nix touched Vahly's shoulder. "Do you want to bury her?"

Vahly shook her head. Somehow, that didn't feel right. Instead, she scooped a handful of earth and set it on the skull. Vahly closed her eyes. The earth's heartbeat tapped her pulse points, and the ground trembled.

Nix sucked a loud breath. Arc whispered Vahly's name as his boots scraped on the grit of the tower floor.

The earth had swallowed the bones, taking the mosaic design with it.

Earth magic.

A tingling spread through her, a wave of power that drove home the fact that she was indeed an Earth Queen.

Mind spinning, Vahly led Arc and Nix outside.

If she was headed into the sea, they needed backup. Amona would send a contingent of warriors if Vahly used the Call to ask. Vahly had hoped to keep this mission small, to avoid others tangling the situation, but it would be madness to go into this without more help.

The path wound down, down, down, and they followed its narrow bends and gentle turns to the water's edge where black rocks crowded the coast and waves rolled over their glassy edges.

Nix stopped, wings twitching in agitation as she eyed the sea. She snarled, then seemed to force herself to walk to the edge of the rocky coastline to stand beside Arc and Vahly. The water couldn't reach her from here unless the sea folk were around to spell it, but just the same, this was a tough thing for a dragon to do.

Vahly wanted to say something to Nix, to thank her again for coming along, but she didn't want to point out Nix's weakness. Nix was obviously finding this situation frustrating enough without further attention brought to her shortcomings.

The wind—salty and inconsistent—bit at Vahly's face as she stared over the flooded ruins of Bihotzetik. Vahly handed her satchel and the egg over to Nix. Nix shouldered the bag, ruffling her injured wing and wincing.

"I'm going to Call Amona," Vahly said. "She can send a few warriors to help keep an eye on us while we're down there."

Nix turned one of her gold and lapis lazuli rings around her scaled finger. Her lips pinched, and she looked like she was ready to argue, but she nodded. "That would be wise. I can't fly just yet."

"Have you tried lately?" Vahly asked.

"Last night. I can do it. But not for long. And not very high." The cost of admitting this was apparent on Nix's face. Vahly wished there were more she could do to help her heal.

Beside them, Arc was already spinning shadows and light around his fingertips, weaving a spell. A fresh breeze lifted the ends of his hair. "I'll cast the spell over you, Vahly. Then we can go into the sea for a brief moment to test its efficacy."

Vahly shut her eyes and focused on Amona. *My matriarch. I need you.*

I am listening.

Vahly startled at the speed of her response. *Thank you. I must go into the sea. Here in Bihotzetik. My magic won't take no for an answer.*

Amona's silence had Vahly picturing her mother's quirked eyebrow and crossed arms.

There is something in the city that I have to find or read or see, Vahly thought to Amona. *I don't want to do it, but Arcturus has magic to help me breathe and swim. We'll be quick and careful. But I'd rather do it with a few of our Lapis warriors keeping watch with Nix.*

I'll take care of it. Wait for our arrival in three days' time. We'll meet at the most southern watchtower. I assume you have spotted the structure?

Yes. Vahly shook off the memory of the skull and the dagger.

They should arrive by nightfall on the third day, Amona said through the bond.

That soon?

I assume you want warriors, not grandfathers.

Vahly laughed. *Indeed.*

So yes. Nightfall. Three days. They will fly as quickly as dragons are able.

Thank you, Mother.

Of course, Daughter.

Vahly opened her eyes and sat beside Arc. She filled him and Nix in on Amona's plans.

Nix sat, tucking her shapely legs up beside her and relaxing her wings so that they spread like a purple-blue veil behind her shadow. "I have something terribly dull to say."

Arc motioned for Vahly to raise her chin. She did so, and his fingertips, dripping in magic, dusted over her lips as he cast the air spell to let her breathe underwater. Her throat tightened, and she thought her heart might come out of her chest—not because of the bizarre magic, but because of the feel of his skin on hers.

His dark eyes gave nothing away. In fact, he made no eye contact at all. Was he avoiding her gaze? His throat moved in a loud swallow, and the scent of him rose into the air. He was enjoying this. She was almost certain. A little teasing wouldn't hurt him.

She grinned and set her hand on the grass beside his thigh, her thumb barely brushing his leg. "Focus, elf. I don't want you to accidentally suffocate me."

Arc met her gaze then, his lids closing halfway. "Behave, Earth Queen." He cocked an eyebrow and pursed his lips as he looked away, speaking spells into the air, taking up where he'd left off.

"So spill, Nix," Vahly said. "Dull sounds nice about now."

The crash of waves on the rocks tumbled past their ears, and Vahly shivered. Her tongue tasted of salt. To fight her growing fear, she breathed in the scent of Arc—sun-warmed tree sap and mint. Her trembling ceased, and she turned her attention to Nix even as Arc continued to work.

Nix stared at the five spires of Bihotzetik that rose from the foaming sea like black talons of a drowned beast. "I'm not going to be much help to you, Queenie."

"Of course you are." Vahly removed her weapons belt, boots, and socks, then took off her vest, readying to go into the water.

"I can't even be your lookout during this first part of our quest." The tip of her blue tongue touched her red lips to wet them. This kind of talk was unlike Nix. She was normally rather full of herself.

Vahly chewed the inside of her cheek. "The hardest part of this whole thing," she said, waving her hands at herself and indicating the changes in her power, "is that I know I'm not the one we truly need. I have no idea what I'm doing, and absolutely every life on land depends on me figuring it out. So please don't say you're no help because you have an injured wing. Stones and Blackwater, Nix. I need you because you're my friend. Just having you to tell me I'm capable of fully waking my magic, being the fabulous and consistent liar you are—that is the greatest help of all."

Arc finished his spellwork and looked down at his hands, a small smile gracing his lips.

Nix shook her head, her lapis lazuli clips glittering in the sunlight as the corner of her mouth lifted. "You *are* fully capable of waking your magic, Vahly. You're already very powerful."

"See?" Vahly elbowed Arc. "Told you she was good at lying. I can barely move a hill of dirt." She held her hands out. "But I'm hopeful. I'll stay positive. With the help of both of you." She stood to climb down the algae-slick rocks toward the ocean.

Nix waved a lazy farewell and took a few steps away from the edge. "Don't take all day."

After removing his boots, surcoat, weapons, and undershirt, Arc followed Vahly.

"Shouldn't I feel the magic on me now, Arc?" Vahly asked.

"Not until you are in the water," he said.

A large wave swelled and rushed over the coastline's rocks, soaking Vahly and Arc to the knee. Whispering a little prayer, Vahly left the ridge of stones and plunged into the home of her greatest enemy.

CHAPTER SIX

Magicked spear in hand, Ryton kicked his legs
through the cool water and twisted to veer
around the southern tip of the bay that now
housed Bihotzetik, the famed city of the previous Earth
Queen.

He'd traveled around the civilization, a good ten miles
from the coast, before circling back to enter the ruins from
the south, not far from where he'd met with the elven spy.
No one could be allowed to spot him, or worse, to follow
him on this quest. Taking the circuitous route ensured that
neither Grystark nor the ambitious, eager-to-please Echo
had trailed him to this place. He wanted to be alone here,
for if he failed, the punishment wouldn't involve his
friends. It'd only be his head on a spear.

The ocean was raucous today, showing off its muscle
and tossing schools of teal jellyfish and orange-striped eels
off their watery paths. The currents at the spit of land
collided, and Ryton dragged his finned arms forward then
back to propel himself through the crossing flows and

onward, into the city's former limits. His coral spear cut through the water, magic shushing around its sharp edge.

He'd never seen a map of the city, but it seemed he'd entered on the less impressive side of town. Small limestone structures showed plain, circular windows and round doorways. A hundred or so of these buildings lined what had once been a road. Ryton swam down to brush the sand and grit away from the gray rocks the humans had fitted like puzzle pieces to form a smooth surface for their land transportation.

Curiosity rising, he dipped into one of the structures to nose around. A school of breaker fish flashed silver, fleeing through the nearest window as he set his spear against the doorframe.

The back wall held three long shelves. Copper pots rusted beside the crumbling remains of a box of knives with handles made of something pale like bone. Antlers.

Yes, he'd seen a human knife once, in a shipwreck. That weapon had also boasted a hilt of antler—the horns of those bounding creatures the humans depicted in their rudimentary artwork. In that shipwreck, he had uncovered a charcoaled mosaic on the wall of the sunken vessel. The trees had shown wide branches and leaves, so similar to the corals that grew near his hometown near Tidehame. Under those trees, the humans had drawn in images of lithe, furred animals with enormous racks of antlers. He had no idea what the humans called the creatures, but they must have been plentiful or sacred, seeing as how many were in that mosaic.

The knife was light in Ryton's grip.

Astraea would see him cut down if she knew he was handling a human weapon.

Lunging, he stabbed at an imagined foe, enjoying the rebellion. Astraea had sent him away, and she was nowhere nearby. He could follow his curiosity on this mission. The freedom left his chest aching though, because it was temporary. The knife slid easily into place on his shell-and-knot belt. He could keep it for a while, but he'd have to give it up after slaying the Earth Queen. When he returned to his people, he would have to hide his interest in human things once again. It was simply not tolerated in sea folk society and especially not in the ranks of the military.

Taking up the familiar weight of his spear, Ryton slipped out of the structure's round door, his hand briefly touching the cold stone. What had they used to fashion these homes of rock? Had their tools been similar to the sea folk's own implements?

A larger building that was missing its roof marked a turn in the road. Inside, eels played chase over the skeletal remains of some twenty humans. A scrap of fabric clung to one skull, and Ryton lifted it from the body. A head decoration of some sort. The edges were mostly eaten away by fish, and only a ragged line of tooled hide remained. Hide was his guess, anyway. Its feel reminded him of a reef whale cloak, the type hunters sometimes wore on their swims into the deepest trenches of the sea. The top of the human item was woven of hair. Short, coarse hair. He touched it again and the fabric fell apart, drifting into the water like powder.

Rectangular tables crowded the rest of the building. A realization spread over him. This was a tavern, not unlike the one he and Grystark frequented. He swam behind the bar and lifted the glass bottles stacked along the wall, one after another. If they'd originally held any of the drink that humans enjoyed, it had all been eaten up by time spent underwater. The bottles were uncorked and unsealed, and they housed only a few snails and inches of sediment.

Ryton returned to the first table and leaned on the rough surface, trying to put himself in the humans' world. What had it been like for them, breathing air and drinking liquids? What had they done in their free time? Had they cast shells like sea folk, betting on their chosen runes to rise to the top? Had those dead ones there played games of chance before the flood took them by surprise?

Wishing he had more time to explore, he wondered if their salt-water-destroyed pockets had given up any fascinating coins or other curiosities. But there was no time for this. He swam out of the tavern and started on his way again.

The worst enemy of his kynd lurked nearby, and it was past time she joined her dead kin to rot at the bottom of the sea.

Venturing closer to the inner circle of the bay, nearer to the coastline, Ryton swam past more one-story houses and a chaotic jumble of what appeared to be shops. Each had a shelf extending from a wide, rectangular window, or at least, the disintegrating remains of one.

An open area in a hexagonal shape stretched beyond the shops. Drifts of both black and white sand blanketed most of the space, but a corner had remained free of grit. Ryton hovered, treading water, to cock his head at what appeared to be another piece of art, not dissimilar to the one he had seen in that sunken ship.

Shades of green, black, and even touches of red—a color the humans rarely used—combined to show a gathering of those trees they had treasured, the ones with the lobed leaves. A plethora of land creatures walked around the leafy growth. Some animals had four legs like the bounding creatures with the antlers, but others had wings. One had both.

Wait. The Watcher had mumbled something about a bird animal called a gryphon. She mentioned it during her last visit to see the queen. Of course, the Watcher was constantly muttering, and most of what she said didn't seem to apply to anything currently happening. Ryton moved more of the sand away from the image of the winged creature. The tree leaves circled the gryphon's head like a crown floating above its dark feathers. Interesting.

The memory of Astraea's fierce order echoed through his mind, and he swam on.

Before he reached the first of the great spires that reached through the water to stand against the waves, a foreign scent tickled his gills. He blew out, bubbles gurgling and rising over his head. What was that? Like seaweed, but not quite the same. Similar to the air he had breathed when he met with the elven spy.

Could it be her, the Earth Queen?

His temples pounded, his blood racing.

Spear at the ready, he flew through the currents, diving, then rising, following the increasing intensity of the scent.

And that's when he spotted his first human.

Strands of golden hair around a strong face. A

determined set to the jaw. Limbs flailing in the worst version of swimming he'd ever witnessed.

Ryton couldn't move. He floated, mouth agape.

The smell of above—unsalted dirt and trees—emanated from her like a strong perfume.

This had to be the Earth Queen.

She blinked, appearing disoriented, as she swam just below the sunlit, pale green surface beside what seemed to be an elf. He swam gracefully, his pointed ears showing against black hair. He smelled like the other elf—of raw air and bright sun—a caustic odor that burned the back of Ryton's throat.

The Earth Queen struggled in the water.

Fire tore through Ryton's temples, and he clenched his teeth. Seas, how he hated her. For what she would do to his kynd. To Grystark and his wife, Lilia.

Ryton's mind painted horrible imaginings.

Grystark screaming for Lilia as this Earth Queen crushed her to death with great stones. He could almost see Lilia's fingers curling in pain, her shout cut off. Grystark's face twisted in grief and shock.

That was what the Earth Queen would do to them if she were allowed to live.

At that moment, Ryton loathed himself for being interested in human culture and artifacts. So what if they did have lifestyles that seemed not too different from his own? It meant nothing. Humans were the enemy, just as dragons. Even if he had not himself witnessed an Earth Queen killing one of his own as he had the dragons, they'd surely done it, time and time again, through the centuries. And this Earth Queen would be no different. Once her powers rose in full, she would attack, and Ryton stood to lose everyone he had left in the world.

Not today, Earth Queen.

Ryton sliced through the water, his vision going red with rage and his lips moving fast through spell after spell. He flew past a blur of structures.

All he had to do was reach them.

Just thirty feet, and he'd be there, his spells choking her, his hands around her throat. He gave no thought to the elf. That creature wouldn't matter. Ryton, in his rage, was a storm unbeatable.

CHAPTER SEVEN

The ocean sucked the warmth from Vahly's bones as she dove. Her eyes burned, unused to the salt.

Arc swam down beside her and moved his hands in and out near his ribs, telling her to try breathing. He was obviously breathing just fine, and his eyes were wide and clear. His magic swirled around his head in blurred ribbons of sun and shadow.

Heart sputtering, Vahly tried to inhale through her nose, but she couldn't make herself do it. It felt like suicide to breathe under water even though she knew Arc's magic would most likely work. Her body simply refused to obey her.

Arc swam close. *I'm right here,* he said into her mind. *If it goes wrong, I will bring you to the surface.*

She leaned into the comfort of his support and, shuddering, forced herself to inhale slowly.

Air flowed into her nostrils and lungs as if she were still above the waves.

Her mouth fell open. "It worked!"

Arc smiled. *Try again.*

More confident now, she inhaled deeply. The air bit at her throat and chest, and she made a face at Arc.

Not as fresh that time? he asked telepathically.

She shook her head and held up a finger. *One more try.*

With a short inhale, the water began to sneak in. Pulse rocketing, Vahly tried to cough, but choked on water. Heat flared inside her chest as Arc's arm circled her from behind.

Kicking powerfully through the water, Arc pulled her above the surface, where the waves slapped Vahly's face. Rocks scraped against her legs, cutting her a thousand times before they reached the shallow water. Once there, on the rocks, Arc helped her get her feet under her.

Vahly's throat was on fire, her eyes not doing much better. Stomach muscles clenching, she coughed, desperate to breathe normally.

Arc twisted healing magic around her like a cloak, its warmth and tingle easing her lungs and eyes. At last, her body was free of ocean water.

"Stones and Blackwater." Salt puckered her tongue, and her throat scratched with every word. "I can't explore the ruins like this."

Arc helped her to the shore where Nix stood clasping her hands.

"I told you this was a bad idea," Nix snapped as she helped Vahly sit on the warm ground.

Overhead, thunder rolled, and the sun disappeared behind a bank of approaching clouds.

Arc raised his air magic, weaving dark and light. He sent a breeze whisking over Vahly like a thousand feathers, drying her clothing for the most part and tossing her hair around. He did the same for himself, then they put their clothing and weapons on.

Arc paced back and forth, his thumb tapping his lower lip and his eyes squinted in thought. "You need some elven blood to make the air magic work. How can we manage that?"

"Are you asking for suggestions?" Vahly coughed as she braided her salt-stiff hair. "Or is this conversation of yours between you and you?"

Nix wiggled a talon. "I can give you a small cut if need be, Arcturus."

He stopped pacing and stared, a grin spreading over his sharp features.

"Why is he smiling about a possible slicing and dicing from a dragon?" Vahly asked Nix.

Nix snorted. "Perhaps the water was spelled, and it boggled his brains."

Arc ignored their teasing. "While we plot, why don't we arrange a camp that's not easily detected?"

Puzzled at what plans he might be concocting in that head of his, Vahly agreed, and the three set off.

CHAPTER EIGHT

R yton was the ocean's fist, the sea's blade, ready to slay that which threatened its glorious depths. But he had failed to catch the Earth Queen.

She had jerked like a fish on a spear, but the elf had grabbed her with both arms and kicked to the surface. With that wild strength the air kynd possessed, the elven male had pulled Ryton's enemy from the water. And just like that, Ryton had missed his chance.

His spelled salt water had choked her, but he'd been too far away to truly injure her. Was the Earth Queen not powerful enough to take a simple swim and fight off a weak spell? Is that why the elf had been forced to rescue her? Or had they seen him and panicked, acting irrationally?

Ryton's heart hammered against his ribs. His legs buzzed, wanting to drive up to the surface, to breach and attempt a crashing wave with spellwork. But if that failed, he'd only alert them to his presence for certain and destroy the possibility that they didn't know he was in pursuit and aware of their location. There were no guarantees a spelled wave would take the human down. No, Ryton needed his hands on her throat, his spear in her gut. A chance at death was not nearly enough.

Gripping his spear, knuckles going white, Ryton shouted his frustration into the water that stretched between him and his quarry. The sound vibrated through the sea like another type of current.

Would it be like that next time? Would he get close but not close enough to secure her demise?

Ryton swam away from the city, toward the deep, open sea, his mind a whirlpool.

The Earth Queen could traverse both land and sea. He was trapped here by what he was. Even if he found some tympanic leaves and managed to get ashore, his time out of water would be severely limited. The lungs in his chest didn't work well enough to remain on land for more than a few minutes, nor could his limbs work in the quick way they would have to in order to destroy the Earth Queen and any others who might aid her, such as the elf.

Had any sea folk ever tried to stay on land for more than a passing moment?

He'd never heard of such a thing.

The Watcher would know.

An idea crept into his thoughts. What if the Watcher knew a way Ryton could access the land and, thus, the Earth Queen? A spelled sphere of salt water, perhaps? Or some type of magic that could help him glean proper oxygen from the raw air? But could she do anything about his body and its dependence on the sea's physical support?

The biggest question of all—the most dangerous

question—was if he did go to the Watcher and ask her, would the Watcher report his failings to Queen Astraea? If she did, he was as good as dead.

Astraea clearly wanted Ryton to quietly destroy the Earth Queen before the sea folk began to panic, the Earth Queen's presence undercutting the confidence and prowess that Astraea and Ryton had worked to build within the great army of the sea.

He swam through a school of grassfish, green and sparkling, each of them twenty feet long with pointed snouts, then dove deep, heading roughly northwest, toward the Watcher's ancient hovel.

The risk was worth the potential reward. The Earth Queen was the sea folk's greatest threat. She could command stone, leaf, and earth, and break the tides and currents, destroying any chance they had of flooding the land. If the Watcher could somehow help him hunt the Earth Queen on land, he could protect his kynd and maybe end this war with the bloodthirsty dragons—creatures who had slain countless sea folk over centuries of ancient feuds —once and for all.

But the Watcher never truly took sides. Her motivations were unknown. Surely, she wanted the sea folk to win. She was one of them, albeit distorted and changed by her divine experience of gaining the Sight. Ryton wondered if the Watcher would decide he was worth the risk of keeping a secret from Queen Astraea or not. What did the Watcher do to folk who didn't fit into her cloaked plans?

THE SEA DARKENED NEAR THE WATCHER'S ABODE. WATER IN

shades of the deepest green flowed through a forest of salt mushrooms, whose muddy stalks and bright crowns towered over a twisting pathway crowded with transparent albino eels.

As Ryton slowed and sank to the sea floor to walk, the eels scattered, their strange orange beaks clacking. He passed under an archway of pitted coral, a dead structure that wouldn't grow larger with time but would become brittle and eventually be carried away by the tides. Not that the currents had much pull down here, in this ditch of a place.

It was quiet, Ryton could appreciate that, but the murky, stale water made it impossible to tell if the shapes floating overhead were detached seaweed or the ghosts of fallen sea folk.

He'd only seen one such spirit in his life, not long after his sister Selene had been killed by the dragons. A pale figure, limbs disturbingly elongated, had drifted past his front door. He had simultaneously hoped it was Selene and prayed it was not. At the time, grief had made him desperate to see her face again, to bid her farewell, to hear her tease him as all siblings do, but he could not stomach the thought that she'd become a distorted ghost.

He hoped and prayed to the Source that she was at peace in her new form, a bright energy suffusing the sea with hope and laughter.

Now, he pushed away the ache of losing Selene to dragons so he could focus on what he would say to the Watcher.

"I hear General Ryton approaching." The Watcher's

ragged voice echoed from the sea cave through the dusky water.

Did she have guests often? Ryton swallowed, wondering if he should have an excuse to cover his visit if someone close to the queen were present.

He entered the mouth of the Watcher's home, keeping his spear lowered. The crone stood over a bowl similar to the one she'd used for scrying in the palace. The sides were steeper than that one though, and a dip along the rim showed the well-worn spot where the Watcher had gripped the edge for the many, many years she had lived and prophesied.

Seaweed unspooled from the walls and ceiling of the cave. Their long leaves cast a peculiar glow over the Watcher's pinched face and the empty places where her eyes had once been. He wondered again if the story about her blinding was true.

"How can I help you, dear general?" The Watcher's voice was a whisper.

Chills snaked down Ryton's back as he set his spear against the wall. He approached with a polite bow. The water flowing closer to the bowl was cold, and it twisted oddly into the vessel, the stone depths catching the cave's glow and distorting a reflection of the Watcher's ancient face.

"I come," he said, "asking for a miracle."

"It is so cold... Dragons of shifting light..." She muttered nonsense until her words became mere sounds and noises.

Ryton didn't know whether to interrupt or stand politely for a while longer. His fins itched to hurry through the water, but he didn't want to upset her and ruin his chance.

"It is as foretold," she said, her voice suddenly loud. "Long shadows still our waters. Or do they blind our army? Not certain. Unclear." The Watcher touched the base of her scrying bowl. "Go on, General."

He cleared his throat and did his best to ignore a chorus of pained moans coming from the back of the cave. She held no spelled prisoners as far as Ryton knew, so the sounds had to be the remnants of some spellwork gone awry.

"I've been ordered to assassinate the last surviving human."

"The Earth Queen. She grows stronger."

"Yes. And to succeed, I must be able to follow her onto land, out of the sea. Is there magic enough to accomplish such a task?"

The Watcher turned and cocked her head as if listening. "Dark magic. There is risk."

"I must try it. If she continues to side with the dragons and I fail in my mission, all is lost."

"Indeed, it is."

She swam toward a set of doors, a shuffling sort of rhythm to her movements. The doors were made entirely of a sickly gray-green shell, a variety Ryton had never seen. The Watcher swung one door open wide and then disappeared inside.

From the room, a shrill shriek pierced the water, raking over Ryton's ears. Temples thudding, he grabbed his spear and followed the Watcher's steps into the dark second room.

"Twist, twist, and twist," she murmured in the inky black.

Ryton's eyes adjusted to the lack of light, and he could just barely see the Watcher as she reached into the opening of a two-foot-wide glass sphere. Then, with a speed that shocked Ryton, the crone swam from the room.

He hurried to follow, bubbles zipping from his lips and running along his cheek. His gut told him to keep his hand on his weapon.

At the scrying bowl, the Watcher faced him and held out a black creature that oozed a sticky-looking substance. The thing was about the size of two of his hands. Long, multi-jointed legs extended from its body. It looked like a trilobite with crab legs, and it clicked in a way that made Ryton shudder.

She pushed it toward him, bubbles rising from her nose and past the scarred skin of her empty eye sockets.

He stepped backward.

"Turn," she ordered.

"Watcher, with all respect, do you swear on your life this will give me the ability to function above water with the same level of skill I have below?"

"No. You will function, but your strength will be lesser. Not by much, as long as you don't remain on land for too long. This creature, born of magicked and bent Blackwater, will sap your own power and will twist it in uncomfortable ways. You must bear the burden if you want the benefits."

"How long will I have up there?"

The crone squinted nonexistent eyes, scarred skin puckering. She tilted her ear upward as if she were listening to someone speaking from far away. Ryton cringed as the black creature clacked and extended its legs, reaching for him as if he were prey.

"It depends on you. Seven days, perhaps."

"Fine. I'll do it."

Turning, he set his jaw to keep from talking himself out of this madness.

The Watcher tugged his shirt up to his neck, and he blinked at her strength. She placed the thing on his upper back, where its cold legs and shelled body sent a shiver rocking across his frame.

Foul magic slithered through his skin like a thousand parasites.

His knees tried to buckle, but he fought the weakness and managed to remain upright.

His only thought was: What have I done?

He'd ruined who he knew himself to be—Ryton the simple sea folk male, general, brother to a fallen sister, friend to an unpredictable warrior. He was now painted in the shades of this creature on his back.

The Watcher sucked water through her pruned lips as she faced him. She set her hands on his shoulders, her fingers touching the tips of the creature's legs. "You will live through this, good general. But for how long? I don't know. I cannot see."

He managed a bow of his head as he worked his shirt over the new burden. His stomach rolled, and he closed his eyes briefly to calm himself. Questions surged into his mind. Would this creature injure him permanently? How was he to remove it? But he bit his tongue. None of it mattered. He had to kill the Earth Queen, and this evil creature would help him do so. He would tackle the rest if, or when, he succeeded with the assassination.

"Thank you for your help, Watcher. The sea realms will be protected because of this spellwork."

"This is not my spellwork, General. Not by my hand was this thing born. Long ago. Another. Another time."

He didn't understand her, but it did not matter.

With one last bow to the crone, he swam from the sea cave, over the stretches of brilliant coral and writhing creatures.

The time had come to properly pursue the Earth Queen and see her dead at his feet, either on land or by sea.

CHAPTER NINE

Vahly spit the taste of ocean water from her mouth as they hiked.

Sloping ground ran from the coastline upward into the hills and mountains. At the base of the game trail they followed, a rock ledge had fallen from the higher elevations to form a shallow cave system. A curtain of akoli grapevines grew over a north-facing opening into the dark shelter. The vines had probably once been tended by Vahly's kynd and used to create the ruby-colored wine she had seen in a few human illustrations in the Lapis library.

The vines tangled and sprouted wild shoots of bright green leaves. Vahly plucked a cluster of the grapes and ate one. Sourness burst over her tongue, and her lips puckered.

Nix took a grape from Vahly's outstretched hand. "If they make you look like that, I'll probably love them."

Nix devoured the rest of the fruit as Arc pushed the vines away from the entrance and disappeared into the cave. Vahly trailed him, grabbing another cluster of grapes.

Light filtered through a space between the fallen ledge and the side of the rocky rise. Fingers of sunlight drew lines across Arc's ebony hair and his strong nose.

"Does this suit you?" he asked, glancing at Nix and Vahly.

Vahly handed him the grapes. "It's good. No rogues would see us from overhead."

She tucked her satchel into a far corner, but as soon as the egg was away from her, an uneasy feeling turned her around. Lifting the pack, she breathed a sigh of relief. The egg would have to stay with Nix on the coast when Vahly went into the sea. The earth magic in Vahly's veins wanted the egg as close as possible.

Arc ate three grapes. "I'm painfully curious about this link you have with your egg."

"Same here. I have no idea what's driving this, aside from my magic. But to what end? What is the point?"

Nix peeled moss from a rock and set it beside more of the green growth near the entrance, creating a bedding of sorts. "It'll be a grand surprise. I almost wish I could find my own little egg to cart about."

Vahly grinned as they left the shelter and returned to the seashore. In full dragon form, dragons laid eggs shortly after mating, but Vahly couldn't imagine Nix dealing with a youngling. She was caring and kind, but she would tire of the constant care they needed.

"Arc, what was it you were thinking earlier?" Vahly asked. "Something about blood?"

Nix sat on a boulder and crossed her legs daintily. Her wings stretched wide, then settled back into place.

Arc crouched by Nix and held out a wrist. "Cut me here, please. It will be much easier if you do it."

Had he lost his mind?

Nix shrugged and swiped a talon across Arc's burnished skin. Bright blood welled along the gash.

Arc turned to Vahly. "May I?" He dipped a finger in the blood on his wrist.

"Uh. Sure?"

Eyebrows drawing together in focus, Arc dotted his blood on each of her temples, her chin, and just above her Blackwater mark.

"This is very dramatic, but I hate to break it to you: I don't feel a thing." Aside from the earth urging her to go back into the sea, of course. That tug was insistent to the point of pain.

"I'll cast the air spell again. I think this time my blood will help it keep a hold on you."

Nix patted the egg inside Vahly's satchel. "Ah. That might work."

"You really think so?" Vahly opened the bag's flap to check on the egg, then closed it again.

"Dragons used to sell the blood of elves," Nix said. "Actually, the vials were filled with pomegranate juice and beetle's blood, and every merchant who dealt in it was a fraud, but still."

Vahly glanced at Arc. "Did you know about this?"

"It does not surprise me." He didn't seem offended, only focused on the task at hand.

"I like that not many things get your hackles up." Vahly patted him on the arm, enjoying the feel of his bicep.

Arc had left off spellwork and instead was perusing the plants in the vicinity. "If one is quick to anger, one wastes too much energy on that which does not improve life."

Nix snorted. "Can I get that on a plaque to put up in the cider house? If my Breakers could get that through their thick heads, I'd save a year's worth of spilled drink over stupid arguments. What are you looking for, Arcturus?" She went to help him, and Vahly joined in.

"There is a plant our children use on their eyes when they go underwater," he said. "It eases the sting of minerals to which their flesh is not accustomed. Once they are five or so, their bodies strengthen and the plant is not necessary for underwater swimming. The plant is called eyewort, and it is dark purple. Grows in bunches."

"Delightful name." Vahly pushed a yellowed shrub aside and found an anthill. "Am I going to have to cram the lovely growth into my eyeballs?"

"I'll create a paste and paint it across your eyelids."

"If it helps with the burning and the clarity of sight, I'm all for *worting* up my vision."

Arc stopped searching and heaved a breath, looking into the higher elevations a few ticks north. "I think we would have better luck looking there."

Vahly nodded, and they gathered the bags to go.

The incline grew steeper as the clouds went black.

Nix muttered something behind Vahly.

"What is it?" Vahly dropped back.

"We are crossing into Jade territory." Nix's pupils shrank as she regarded Vahly, her stare loaded with warning.

Arc bent to check a cluster of dark green flowers. "And you are worrying about those rogue Jades."

"I am," Nix said.

Vahly sped up, taking the lead toward the very top of the rise.

They spread out, searching the patches of growth between the rocky expanses and boulders. The storm had drifted back out to sea, but it would return. It had that kind of twisting wind to it.

"I'm going to fill our water skins." Vahly said. "Why don't you two rest?"

A fallen branch lay under an olive tree that had been stripped of its lower leaves by an animal, a deer perhaps. Vahly took the skins from Arc and Nix, then hung them from the branch and set it across her back.

"You are certain you don't want company?" Arc bit off a corner of bread from his pack. Chewing, he lifted an eyebrow at her in question.

"I need some time to breathe."

Nix gave her a smile, sat, and began to rub her right calf. "Keep a low profile, Queenie."

Nodding, Vahly headed toward a stretch of low shrubs and mossy stones that spoke of water.

The mountain range extended in all directions from her vantage point. Shades of hickory and slate undulated toward the faraway Jade palace, the peaks growing more jagged the farther north they went. A hazy line of pale landscape showed the pass that led into the remote northern lands, just east of the Jades' home. No one lived that far north because nothing grew there and prey was scarce.

There were times when an empty territory sounded perfect to Vahly.

At least in a place like that, she'd be able to sleep without keeping one eye open.

Shaking off her mental fatigue, she shoved through the low growth and found the spring wetting the bright green moss at her feet. She wouldn't have a good night's sleep for a long, long while, if ever, and there was no use whining about it.

VAHLY RETURNED TO NIX AND ARC, HER BACK ACHING. THE water skins swinging from the long branch across her shoulders sloshed. When she spotted them, she jerked to a stop.

Nix, in her human form, blew dragonfire at Arc.

One water skin slid free and plopped onto the ground.

Heart snapping in fear, Vahly dropped the branch and the rest of the skins and ran.

"Nix!"

What could have happened to destroy their relationship in the time she'd been gone?

Arc had his back to Vahly. He held up a hand. "It's all right. Stay back, please."

Nix's fire had lessened in strength at Vahly's shout, but she increased its intensity now. The air filled with crackling pops. Wind rushed past Vahly's ears, and the smell of dragon magic combined with Arc's natural, elven scent.

The tongues of dragonfire spooled around twisting fingers of light and dark air magic. The elements created an eddy of power.

What were they up to?

Vahly wiped her sweating palms on her trousers.

If Nix raised her head just a few inches, Arc would be roasted. Vahly didn't think Nix would intentionally hurt him, but accidents happened in the realm of dragons. Lots of accidents.

"Down," Arc called out, his hands held apart, his fingers curling above the gust and snap of their combined magic.

They directed the whirling mass of fire and color toward the ground.

Chunks of dirt, prickly snakeweed, and tiny rocks flew from their creation, but most of the ground dissolved into black smoke on contact.

Vahly stepped closer. A rock pinged against her cheek, but she kept on. Her ears roared with the noise.

"So much for keeping this quest quiet," she called out, hands extended in a gesture of helplessness.

The rogues would hear this chaos if they were anywhere nearby. Half of her wanted to look over her shoulder in case they were already approaching, barreling toward them with talons out and fire blazing. But the other half of her was far too entranced with this new magic to turn away for even a moment.

Arc lifted his hands and met Nix's gaze, and as one, they ceased their spellwork. The easy sounds of sea, breeze, and birds reigned again.

Vahly rushed over.

Between them, a great hole extended into the earth, deep enough to hide all three of them, one on top of the other.

Nix dusted her hands and smoothed her hair. "That was

decidedly not dull, Arcturus. In fact, I might now be quite in love with you and your ridiculously creative mind."

Vahly crouched to touch a scorched stone at the edge of the pit. A surprised laugh bubbled out of her. "Arc, if we do survive the Sea Queen, do you know how much gold the dragon guilds will pay for this magic? They can fire-drill into rock just fine, but earth? They have a tough time with digging out earthworks. You'll be as rich as Amona."

She stood and patted his shoulder. He was practically glowing with what she assumed was happiness at what his experiment had wrought.

"If you live through all the horrors I'm sure to heap on you, that is," she added.

Arc flexed his fingers, and his excited gaze locked onto her. "We should repeat this trial with your earth magic, then compare the results."

Nix lounged on a patch of verdigris-hued plants, adjusting her wings to avoid the nearby snakeweed. "He doesn't seem to care about his potential fortune, Vahly. I suggest we get his apathy on this issue in writing." She winked at Arc.

Vahly's cheeks lifted in a smile. Here was another glimpse of the old Nix, more valuable than any measure of coin.

"How can we use this to fight the sea folk?" she asked Arc.

"I don't have any solid ideas on that yet. But are you willing to try our three magicks together?"

"Definitely."

"It may result in an unwieldy storm of power."

"Oh!" Nix brushed her sleeve free of debris. "Can that be your nickname for me?"

Arc raised one dark eyebrow. "Aren't nicknames supposed to be shorter than one's given name?"

"Pssssh." Nix waved a hand. "You and your rules." Her stomach growled.

"Stones, Nix," Vahly said. "You inhaled three deer last night. How on earth are you hungry?"

"Experimenting with dangerous elven magic demands that one consume a full herd of deer."

"I do hope not." Arc chuckled and patted his own flat stomach.

"Your lesser digestion capabilities are not my problem," Nix said.

"But your greater stomach needs might well become his if you are too tired to hunt," Vahly joked.

Nix rolled onto her stomach and set her chin on her folded arms. Her scales threw sunlight toward the sky. "I believe Arc has been holding back on his abilities with those throwing knives. Now, scurry off, my lovelies, and slaughter all the adorable animals in the vicinity for me."

Arc shook his head, grinning. "Such a ghastly beast." He helped Vahly pick up the water skins she had dropped.

"And, Blackwater curse me, how I adore her," Vahly said.

They started off again, searching for the plant Arc wanted to use on Vahly.

Two boulders the size of Amona in full dragon form hulked over what looked like a small spring, complete with a few thickly leaved trees and an area of high grass.

Vahly scanned the area, keeping an eye out for the Jade

rogues. "Perhaps if the rogues spot me with all this blood on my face, they'll think twice about threatening us."

"They should," Arc said.

Vahly huffed. "Ha. They're dragons."

"I said *they should*. Not that they *would*."

"I heard that." Nix flew into sight and landed behind Arc.

"Weren't you going to take a nap?" Vahly wouldn't have blamed her, what with the healing wing and all. She seemed to be flying fairly well though.

Nix waved a hand, her rings sparkling. "I couldn't let you have all the fun."

The spring gurgled as the wind picked up, smelling like sea and metal. The coming storm kicked dust and fallen leaves around Vahly's legs and into her eyes. She rubbed her face, then bent to search the area below an olive tree.

"See anything?" Vahly asked Arc.

Lightning cracked, making Vahly jump. She glanced at Nix, who was staring into the sky wistfully. Nix had to be wishing she were up there in the lightning, relishing her fire magic's secondary source.

"I see what might be the correct plant." Arc pointed beyond the boulders to a hill covered in the color of bruises.

"That's eyewort?" Vahly handed her pack to him, then scaled the nearest boulder to get a better view. It was a similar color to the vivanias she'd plucked from the cliffs on a day that felt very long ago indeed.

Beside the plants and their hill, a flash of bright emerald green showed in a rocky pass.

Vahly's heart seized.

A chill ran down her back.

A Jade dragon? She flattened herself on the boulder. She hadn't seen enough to know if it had just been a blowing cluster of leaves, a Jade in human-like form, or a fully shifted dragon.

Vahly? Arc said inside her mind. *Is it the rogues?*

If it was, we are in a heap of trouble.

CHAPTER TEN

I *may have seen one Jade dragon. Let me watch for a minute,* Vahly said telepathically to Arc.

The wind gusted. Rain began to splatter, creating large circles on the boulder around Vahly and wetting her recently dried hair.

Lightning cracked.

No more possible Jades appeared, so she climbed back down to where Nix and Arc waited. Arc handed over her satchel, and Vahly settled it across her body.

Nix's wings shuffled, and she sniffed the air. "I can't scent any dragons. Not with this storm."

Rain streamed down in sheets, and thunder shook the ground like a herd of enormous deer were headed their way. Nix stretched her wings over all three of them, creating an amethyst ceiling with sapphire beams.

Hands fisted, Vahly watched the area that surrounded the boulders. Arc cleared his throat, and she jumped, thinking a rogue was about to leap from the storm. This weather was terrible for scouting, searching for plants, and for magic.

"I don't think I can test out your blood and your plant in this weather, Arc," she said. "The waves would swallow me whole even if we managed the magic. Let's go back down and rest."

"And eat." Nix licked her lips, her azure tongue like the bottom of a flame. "When in doubt, eat. I still have some of the bacon plant in my bag. If you massage my injured wing, I might be inclined to share." She walked between Arc and Vahly, keeping them somewhat sheltered from the blowing storm.

Vahly glanced backward, but now she couldn't see around Nix to watch for Jades. She slid out of her friend's shelter. "I'll watch our backs. You two go on. Just in case that wasn't my imagination up there."

Rain darkened the sandy ground and splashed against the wide leaves of a tuberous succulent.

Vahly's satchel rubbed against her neck as she walked behind Arc and Nix. Every few steps, Vahly turned to look into the pouring rain. Lines of gray water rushed to the earth, hiding everything more than arm's length from her face and muddying the path. Water began to seep into her boots despite the coating of balm she'd applied before leaving the Lapis mountain palace.

The paths down to sea level forked—the way they had come twisted through an open area, free of boulders and growth, while the other was a narrow passage through two rock formations reminiscent of great fists. Weak light showed from the pass, indicating the opening extended all the way through.

They tucked themselves into a cluster of olive trees for cover, and Vahly patted the egg inside her pack. She sighed as she ran a hand all along its rounded form, checking for any damage. The egg seemed well enough so far. It simply *had* to hatch. Her heart squeezed with a love that truly made no sense. Shaking her head at herself, she drew a slow breath to calm her pulse. She couldn't handle the thought of this little creature being gone from the world.

Under the sparse olive leaves, rain dripped between Nix's wings. Droplets slid down Nix's forehead and over the thick lashes of her yellow eyes. Arc was soaked too, and the water only made him look more otherworldly as it glistened against his skin.

Vahly wiped a chill hand over her face to clear it of water. "I think we should take the passage there." The waterfalls pouring off the rocks drowned her voice. She pointed between the giant knuckles of stone. "Less chance of an ambush, because we'll be hidden from view. I would hate to stroll right through an open field," she said more loudly. "I'll go out first."

"No. You are the most valuable. When will you accept that?" Nix tsked. "I'll go out first, and if the rogues hit me, you'll know to act. It's not going to be easy for me to force my way through though, not with these beauties." Her wings shivered, and she slapped a thigh proudly.

Without another word, she headed into the narrow passage, her wings stretched wide like she was flying sideways through the opening.

Vahly's stomach twisted, and imaginary needles pricked the back of her neck. She set her jaw and tried not to worry.

"Go ahead, Vahly." Arc nodded toward the passage, his lips wet with rain.

She touched his chest, her fingers pressing into the fine cloth of his surcoat and feeling the muscle and bone beneath. "Please keep all your fancy elven magic blazing strong. I don't have a good feeling about this."

"Should we get Nix and go back the other way? The way we approached?"

"No. This way is less exposed than that wide-open death meadow. I think. I hope." Cursing under her breath, she followed Nix into the pass.

The rain disappeared as the stone hands welcomed Vahly. The smell of Nix's magic mixed with the scent of rain and cave. Vahly's knee scraped the rock wall, tearing her trousers and sending a line of pain across her skin, and she bit her lip, hissing before she continued shuffling along. Her boots squelched in the mud as Arc called her name behind her.

"Are you all right?" The passageway cloaked his face in near darkness.

Vahly blinked and glanced to the side to glimpse his magic. "I'm fine."

The passageway rose under their sodden boots, then turned northward. Thunder shook the air and lightning flashed, showing the exit beyond the shape of Nix's sideways form.

Vahly's warm breath bounced off the rock before her, easing the chill on her chin and cheeks. Her hands spread over the rock at her back, steadying her. The magic inside her was quiet for the moment. She wondered if it was because they were in danger. Or perhaps that was just how the magic worked, waxing and waning with her purpose and energy levels. She knew so little about her power, about herself.

A loose stone rolled beneath her boot, and she jerked. Her bag fell forward and hit the stone wall with a sickening thud.

Her heart seized.

Sweating, she frantically felt around the egg's shape, checking it. The back of her tongue tasted bitter. If it was broken ...

Her magic surged inside her, and she gasped.

"Vahly!" Nix and Arc called to her in unison.

Eyes closed, she fought to keep from crying or screaming or exploding—whatever it was her magic was trying to do to her. She felt like a cracking egg herself, her power trying to burst from the shell of her body. She drew in a deep breath, her pulse racing as power flooded her veins and thrummed deep in her chest like a caged animal. Swallowing, she fought to stay in one piece.

"What is happening to me?" she croaked.

Arc and Nix touched her shoulder, her arm, her hand. Her skin seemed to soak in their warmth.

"I don't know, but we're here. We won't leave you," Arc said.

"You'll handle it, Vahl," Nix whispered. "You're a queen, and don't you forget it."

Tears burned Vahly's eyes, but she held them back as the vicious trembling died away. The walls of the pass held her up—without them, she would've been on the ground. She took two slow breaths, smiling weakly at her companions.

Finally, with one more long inhalation, she began to feel somewhat normal.

With shaking hands, she managed to flip the satchel's flap open. Her fingers danced over the egg, first one side, then the other, the passageway severely restraining her movement. The egg was well and whole, and Vahly smiled like a fool to know it.

"It's not broken." She exhaled in a rush. "I thought I'd cracked it. I tripped."

Arc's shoulders dropped as he too relaxed. "Do you need me to tend to your knee? I might be able to despite these less than ideal surroundings."

"No, I'm fine. We need to get out of this tomb. Nix, if you don't mind?"

"Don't have to tell me twice. I think I prefer almost anything to this place." Her body scraped along the rock, nearing the exit.

The lightning washed the passage in silver.

"Anything?" Vahly asked, putting a hand to her hilt in preparation for leaving the sheltered pass. "Even Lapis nobility genealogy ceremonies?"

"Oh, Stones. Do you think I ever even witnessed one of those monstrosities? I have a life, Vahly. Well, I did before you dragged me into the wilderness."

"If we get out of this alive and the world doesn't end, I'll be sure to invite you to one. It'll set your bar for entertainment so low, you'll never think anything is horrible ever again."

"Stop threatening me with torture, Queenie. I may be bound to serve you, but I don't think suffering Lapis snobbery is part of the deal."

Vahly coughed a laugh as they approached the end of the passageway.

Nix maneuvered her way out, wings tipping and curses stringing through the sound of thunder.

Vahly glanced back at Arc only to realize he wasn't there. She opened her mouth to call out to him—

A full-sized Jade dragon knocked Nix to the ground.

The rogue dragon smiled into the darkness.

CHAPTER ELEVEN

Vahly raged out of the passageway, arms scraping against the rocks and heart punching up into her throat.

The dragon barked what might have been a mocking laugh, the rain pelting his moss-green scales and the membrane of his outstretched wings.

Vahly's sword pierced through the pouring rain, and just when she could've shoved the point toward the soft spot in on the dragon's groin—a place he would certainly block with ease—she turned to surprise him, swinging the blade under the rogue's wing joint.

The steel bit into the dragon's flesh.

He fell back, then lunged at her, his fiery, slitted eyes flashing. A razor-sharp talon raked across Vahly's chest, then struck out horizontally again, this time missing her. A deep burning seared her flesh, and blood poured down her shirt between her breasts from the dragon's first strike.

Dragonfire erupted from the rogue's open maw.

Every inch of Vahly buzzed as she ducked in what

seemed like a slowed version of time, her free hand covering the egg inside her pack as if she were a gryphon mother. Her gut clenched, and her heart screamed for the innocent creature inside. Dragonfire rippled—sapphire and citrine—the flames bright as jewels overhead. The heat, unhindered by the rainstorm, drew sweat from every pore on Vahly's body.

A battle cry tore the air behind her.

Rotating in a crouch, she watched Arc raise an air magic wind that blasted the silver spears of rain away from his outstretched arms and pressed the dragonfire toward the Jade.

The creature shrieked. His fire died.

The air magic pushed against Vahly, and, wincing, she fell onto her injured knee. The wind circled, whirled, then dragged both her and Arc away from the rogue Jade before dropping them to the wet earth.

Nix leapt to her feet, her face cloaked in mud, eyes like suns breaking through the storm. She stumbled toward the rogue Jade. "This is the Earth Queen, fool! She's trying to save your arse from the sea!"

The Jade twisted and threw a glare at Nix. His great tail lashed at Vahly and Arc, who flattened themselves to keep from being struck with a deadly blow.

The dragon shifted to his human-like form in a flash, faster than she'd seen any dragon change.

His voice snapped through the sound of thunder. "Call me fool again, Lapis worm!" His voice was rough from the sudden shift. Lightning cracked, and he drew the sort of breath that preceded dragonfire.

Nix held up her hands. "I'm no Lapis. I'm a Call

Breaker. *The* Call Breaker. Mistress of the Cider House of Dragon's Back. If you rain your fire down on me, every Breaker on this island will hunt you down."

Vahly sheathed her sword. The earth's heart thudded in echo to her own pulse, the beat that shuddered through the cut beneath her collarbone.

The rogue dragon's nostrils bled night-dark smoke.

He was going to attack again.

Drenched to the bone and bleeding freely, Vahly bent and dug her fingers into the sandy mud. The grit pushed beneath her fingernails, and she welcomed the feel of it, the scent of the world supporting her, holding her.

"Rise," she called to the earth.

The ground trembled as if a great clap of thunder had rolled through.

But this was her power. Not the storm's.

A circle of the earth rose around the rogue dragon, bringing a salt cedar shrub with blood-red blooms and a tangle of long-since-forgotten akoli grapevines with it.

Nix's smile was white in the storm's gray light.

"Defend," Vahly whispered to the earth before her.

A tremor shook her bones, and the storm nearly blew her backward as the beat of the world thundered in time with the angry sky.

Arc stood beside Vahly, eyes wide.

The ground piled upon itself to form a circular barrier around the rogue.

And then it fell, crashing, pressing, shoving the enemy dragon into the ground.

The rogue's terrible roar was cut off with a finality that

could only mean death. Lightning washed the mountain pass and the new grave.

A spasm shook Vahly, and her teeth chattered enough to make her jaw ache. Her knees jellied. She fell, all her energy drained from using her new magic.

The rain departed like a crowd finished with the entertainment at hand.

"Not bad, Queenie."

Vahly wanted to feel triumph, but only a hollowness filled her, a shade of the sadness that haunted her since the death of Dramour, Ibai, and Kemen.

Arc put a warm, strong hand on Vahly's back. "It was necessary."

Her eyes shuttered at the gentle contact, and she imagined soaking in Arc's kind words. With a deep breath, she was able to nod in silent gratitude.

"Stones, yes, it was." Nix blew a bit of dragonfire over the dead and buried rogue. "He would've killed at least one of us if it came to more fighting. What a maniac. No manners whatsoever." She crouched by Vahly, her gaze darting from Vahly's cut to her face.

Arc moved the partially ripped neckline of Vahly's shirt, then let his hands hover over the jagged talon cut on her chest. Tingling warmth eased into her flesh. The blood stopped flowing, but the pain lingered.

Something was wrong. Very wrong.

"I'm hurt," she said dumbly, her ears ringing.

"Yes." Arc traded a pinched look with Nix.

Nix brushed Vahly's hair from her forehead with a cool, damp hand. "Arcturus is healing you. I'm guessing the magic you did sucked you dry. What do you think, Arcturus? Don't you think that's really the big issue here?"

"I do. You aren't accustomed to wielding your earth magic. It'll take time and practice to grow strong enough to withstand the toll it takes on your human body and soul."

"Does magic drain elves, too?" Nix asked.

Arc finished his healing work. "It does. When I was younger, the magic exhausted me. But after much training, I seem to remain unfazed by using great amounts of magic." He plucked a soft, unusual leaf from where it sprouted beneath another salt cedar shrub and dabbed it along the dried blood of Vahly's cut.

She took the leaf from him with gentle fingers. "Thank you, Arc. I've got it from here."

Her body was still shaking, and her ears rang with the knowledge that something was off, but she couldn't sit here forever. Perhaps moving on—back to the ruins in the sea—would ease the feeling. Perhaps her magic was urging her to get under the sea as quickly as possible.

She cleaned the blood away as best she could and straightened her vest, and they headed down the mountain.

Their voices mingled in low tones, talking of the rogues and how Vahly's magic might work against the sea folk.

"I could raise a small island in the ocean, perhaps." Vahly stepped beneath two olive trees, their leaves dripping from the earlier storm. "But I'll most likely pass out right afterward, so I'm not sure how helpful that is."

"My kynd could leap to your new islands," Arc said.

"I said one island. Don't get too excited."

"When you grow stronger—which you will—and you create several new islands, my kynd could use them as a base from which to throw spellwork farther away from shore. We can blind the sea folk temporarily by darkening the sea to black, then washing it in bright light. Their eyes are far more sensitive than ours."

Nix plucked an olive from another tree and popped it between her lips. "If your islands are large enough, and you wall them up like you did to that rogue, we dragons could be further protected from salt water the sea folk spell with their spears and chanting. We could use the earth creations as bunkers between strikes."

Arc's eyes flashed. "And I could drive back the salt water near the land bunkers as the dragons lift off again. This could truly work."

Vahly shook her head to try to stop her ears from ringing. She touched her pack, feeling for the egg, for the strange comfort it gave her.

"I love your enthusiasm," she said, "but the Sea Queen can raise waves taller than a respectable mountain. My islands would have to be enormous. How can I possibly—"

Her heart stopped.

The pack was flat as a cooking stone.

Empty.

Her stomach heaved, and she fought to stay upright.

"Vahly?" Arc was at her side in a flash of movement, Nix just behind him.

"The egg." Vahly's trembling fingers lifted her satchel to show a ripped seam along the bottom. The rogue's second strike must have torn the pack open. "It's gone."

CHAPTER TWELVE

Vahly's throat seized up. She fought to breathe, panic beating fists against her ribs. "The egg must have fallen out during the fight."

She was already running on weak legs back up the mountain. The sun glared down, drawing the moisture from Vahly's hair and clothes.

Behind her, Arc's breaths came hard, but his feet made no sound. "We'll find it."

"He's right." Nix flew to catch up with them, her wings blocking the sun and casting a dusky shadow over Vahly. "We haven't been gone but for a few minutes. It'll be there."

"And the ground is soaked, so its landing was most likely soft," Arc said.

His gaze was focused on the next turn in the trail, eyebrows knitted, mouth pinched up to one side. For a moment, Vahly was distracted from sheer terror at losing this egg that oddly meant so much. Arc had known her for such a short time, but her needs had become his.

She swallowed a lump in her throat. "It's good to have a royal elven warrior at my side."

"Fat lot of good it'll do having one elf if we run into a gang of these Jade rogues," Nix hissed, pointing and pulling Vahly to a stop.

The top of a head bobbed beyond the turn, over the smooth, quickly drying boulders. Pale hair, a slip of green scales—a Jade-blooded dragon in human-like form.

Vahly gripped Nix's arm. "It's them."

Nix huffed. "Well, it's not Amona's reinforcements."

The dragon disappeared from view.

Arc leaned closer to Nix and Vahly. "Let's climb that grassy knoll and do a count," he whispered. His magic swirled around his temples, and Vahly tried to take strength from his powerful presence and his royal elven blood.

"Agreed."

She was the first to scale the small rise, pulse pounding in her ears.

Peeking through foot-tall plank grass, she could see eight dragons around a stack of tree limbs most likely gathered for firewood. One dragon, with his sage-hued scales and wide jaw, seemed familiar. Vahly was almost certain she'd met him at some point in the past. The dragon beside him had pale hair, tied into a queue at the back of his neck.

The pale-haired dragon turned, possibly hearing the shuffle of Nix's wings as she spread them low along the ground to keep them out of sight. His eyes were a bright lavender, a rare trait seen only in dragons with Jade blood.

Nix met Vahly's gaze. Vahly jerked her chin at the first

dragon—the one with the sage scales—as if to ask *Do you remember this dragon?*

Nodding, Nix shimmied back down and waved for Arc and Vahly to do the same.

Before following Nix's suggestion, Vahly watched the dragons, making sure the sage-colored one hadn't seen them. But the rogue went back to collecting wood. They were setting up camp, building a fire. A third male—this one with three thick, hickory-brown braids—dropped a full-grown ram beside the stack of firewood. Sometimes dragons enjoyed using their own fire to cook their food, but usually they used wood for roasting food. Controlling dragonfire to a degree that would cook and not burn the food was difficult.

They obviously had no knowledge that Vahly had killed one of their own just down the way. It was possible they had traveled via the northwest passage through this range and had yet to discover the pile of earth that covered their dead cohort.

Guilt stabbed Vahly for a moment before her agony over the egg reigned once more in her heart and soul.

Then she saw it.

The egg sat, partially upright, against the wall of rock that hemmed in the pass. That must have been where it fell from Vahly's satchel. Rolling to her back, she squeezed her hand into a fist and pressed it into her aching stomach. Tilting her head, she checked the egg again. Its deep plum-colored specks glistened with raindrops that must have drizzled from the olive tree growing out of the rocks above. Everything in Vahly demanded that she leap from this hiding place, annihilate every creature in her way, and shield the egg with her own body.

Nix tugged on her boot, her eyes narrowed.

Vahly climbed down. "The egg is there," she whispered. "Beside what looks like the beginnings of a camp. I don't think they've seen the egg yet, but they will. It's huge. And they're dragons."

"And that means?" Arc cocked his head and slicked his wet hair off his forehead.

"They're hungry," Nix whispered. "Dragons are always hungry. Haven't you learned that yet? And you call yourself a man of science."

Vahly took a slow, deep breath to keep from losing her mind. "So you recognize the sage dragon with the wide jaw too?" she asked Nix.

"I do. He was a palace guard, the one we paid off when we smuggled that sharkstone out of the Jades' lesser treasury."

"Oh. The stuff we used to reinforce the ocean-facing wall of the city of thieves in case of a sea folk attack."

"Exactly. He took his coin like a good boy. He adores gold, and we paid him well for turning his eye away from our little project."

All dragons loved gold, loved lying in it, rolling around in it, breathing in its metallic scent. But some dragons became obsessed with the stuff. It was like a powerful herb to them, driving them mad with glee. Amona called that type weak, but the Call Breakers had their own term for it—*binger,* one who binges on gold. They tended to find others like themselves and grow close, their shared obsession binding them like an oath.

"I'm guessing he's a binger." Nix clicked her tongue, thinking, while Arc kept a keen eye out for the rogues. "We can use that."

"We don't have any coin on us. But we could claim we're on our way to a well-paying job at the Jades' palace. Get him in on it somehow?" Vahly forced herself to breathe normally, but her head pounded, and her thoughts whirred in dizzy, nonsense circles like a smacked mosquito.

Arc glanced at her, his eyes pinched with worry. "Why not simply explain the situation and how you're the only one who might be able to fight the Sea Queen and save the island? It seems ludicrous that they wouldn't side with us."

Vahly sighed. "We'll try it if they react in a non-ludicrous way. But I'm guessing a pack of rogue dragons whose alcohol I can smell from here is not going to be reasonable."

"She's right." Nix stopped pacing and regarded Arc and Vahly in turn, her lips turning up at the edges. "If they seem like they might listen to our improbable tale and perhaps watch a demonstration of your magic, then we'll go that route. If they're a bunch of thick-headed louts, we'll use the Jade job lie. And we'll just casually notice the egg. We'll make an offer. I know a Jade youngling with a penchant for rarities like a gryphon egg. His father is a wealthy noble who would pay three times what the egg would be worth to anyone else."

The ache in Vahly's head faded, and she returned Nix's sly smile. "It's a plan."

SHARPENING HIS KNIVES, ARC HUNG BACK IN CASE THEY

needed reinforcement. Explaining the presence of an elf would only make the con more difficult. These rogue Jades most likely still believed elves to be extinct and wondered what kind of foul magic was at play. Or the rogues might decide he was valuable and worth auctioning off to some Jade with whom the rogues remained in contact.

Nix led Vahly into the rogues' camp, hips swaying and feet delicately picking their way along the game trail's sandy rocks and salt cedars.

Vahly's eyes longed to glance at the egg, to check if it sat where she'd seen it moments ago, but she forced herself to play her role.

The pass opened to show a crackling fire and the rogues gathered loosely around a makeshift spit. The sage dragon turned the skinned ram over the flames.

Nix feigned surprise and touched the ruby necklace at her throat. "What is this?" She used that husky voice males loved. "A bevy of handsome fellows in the middle of nowhere? How lovely!"

A lightness filled Vahly, helping her bear the weight of worry about the egg. This was the Nix she knew, the dragon unshadowed by grief—confident and charming. Of course, Vahly would never begrudge Nix her mourning, but her inconsistent behavior was worrying, and seeing this transformation back to how she once was heartened Vahly greatly.

"Greetings, fellow travelers." Vahly's gaze ripped along the ground, searching for any glimpse of plum-hued spots or soft, smooth surfaces, to see if they'd already found the egg and planned to devour it.

The pale-haired dragon stood and whipped the

weather-worn edges of a chestnut-colored cloak away from his sword arm. The hilt of his blade was ivory like Vahly's.

"Halt," he said, his lavender eyes bright.

Nix waved him off and sniffed the roasting meat. "Don't worry, love. We're no threat to you and your mighty assembly here." Her gaze went to the sage dragon. "Luc! Oh, it is good to see you. How have you been? I didn't realize you'd given up your post as palace guard."

Luc. Yes, that was his name. The middle-aged dragon cocked his head at Nix, then ran a gnarled hand over his wide jaw. His scales reflected the afternoon's final sun rays, light that pierced the retreating storm front's charcoal clouds.

"You know this dragon?" the pale-haired male demanded. His words held the command of a leader.

"I do, Baz. This is Nix of the Dragon's Back. She leads the Call Breakers there, near the clanless city, and runs the cider house. I looked the other way when her band of thieves stole sharkstone from the lesser treasury."

Baz narrowed his rare eyes on Nix and Vahly. "And did you pay my friend here well for risking his life for your personal gain?"

Nix smiled at another male, a gangly fellow who looked like he should've been young but had the wear and tear of age. The male scooted to the far side of the log he'd taken as a seat, and Nix settled herself beside him like it was the most normal thing in the world to cozy up to dangerous strangers.

"Why don't you tell him about our deal and how it went for you, dear Luc?" she asked, a purr in her throat as she eyed the sage dragon. "He'd believe you over me, I presume."

Every one of the dragons stared at Nix, their mouths slightly agape and their eyes half-slitted.

"She paid me handsomely, Baz." Luc offered Nix a bladder of what smelled like alcohol, but it wasn't cider or wine.

An acrid scent wafted from the container. The stuff could probably clean the rust off a one-hundred-year-old blade.

Nix took a swig without spilling a drop or blinking an eye. She nodded in thanks and handed the bladder back to Luc. Luc tied the bladder to the pack sitting at his feet, glancing at Baz with reticence in his eyes.

"Hmm." Baz crossed his arms. The bronze-studded gauntlets on his forearms caught the fire's light. "Make a heart oath that you won't reveal our whereabouts to either the Jade or the Lapis matriarch."

Vahly gritted her teeth. Nix couldn't make that promise. Who knew when the information would be useful during their quest? It wasn't worth the risk. But how could they get around making this oath?

Nix frowned and leaned forward. "Are you not Jades yourselves?" she asked Baz, then studied Luc, feigning ignorance of their identity as rogues, as Amona had informed. "Don't tell me you are Call Breakers like myself now?" She widened her eyes and smiled.

"We are," Baz said. "But we don't care to work for you. With all due respect." He shut his eyes for a moment and tipped his head in a nod that reeked of mockery.

Vahly's teeth ground together. "Who says she would

have you?" She stood ready to reach into the dirt at her feet, to access the earth's power, but she hoped it wouldn't come to that, because her head was spinning, and she'd most likely pass out before she proved anything to anyone.

Baz glared but otherwise ignored Vahly's barb. "I suppose you're Matriarch Amona's fancy little pet, hmm? I heard about you when I was a lad, before I came to these mountains and broke the Call."

So he definitely didn't know she had washed in the Blackwater, nor did he seem to realize that every other dragon on the island had sworn allegiance to her.

Vahly looked at Nix. Should they try to explain who she was? Nix gave her a head bob.

Vahly blew out a breath, her palms sweating. "Baz, you're a little behind on news. It sounds impossible, but I'm finally living up to this." She pointed to the Blackwater mark between her eyebrows. "I think I can help us all fight the sea folk."

Everyone froze.

Baz was the first to step toward Vahly, smoke drifting from his nostrils. "Do you think I'm a fool? That if you give me a sweet story about saving the world, I'll feed you at my fire and welcome you in, bowing and scraping to gain your favor? Well, I'm not."

Stones, he reminded her of Maur. Ugh.

"No bowing necessary." Vahly set her palms on the damp ground. A stag beetle crawled past her thumb, and the sandy earth rubbed against her skin. Her ears rang, and she winced at the pain.

"I don't mind your bowing, Baz, if you feel so inclined," Nix said, giving him a wink.

Using Nix's distraction, Vahly focused on the earth.

A rumble sounded from the ground below Baz's feet.

He jumped back, throwing a curse at her. The dirt mounded into a shape, a fist perhaps.

An echo to Vahly's own fist five steps away?

She raised her eyebrows at this new development even as fatigue, the ache of using magic, and her worry for the egg pushed her onto her backside.

"What is this?" Baz snarled.

"I told you. I'm the Earth Queen. I wasn't lying in hopes for a bite of meat."

Nix cleared her throat. "She is our savior and will make good on that mark she wears if we only support her. Now, Baz. I cannot make another heart promise. Is it all right if I call you by the name?" She didn't wait for him to give her permission but soldiered on. "I have three oaths upon me now. I won't take another, but you know where I dwell. At the cider house. On Dragon's Back. You can find me and slay me any time you wish to try it should I reveal your territory. Which I won't. It wouldn't serve me to begin snitching on dragons when I'm the worst criminal of you all."

"She makes good sense," Luc said, his gaze straying to Nix's hips.

"Why don't we eat and talk more about it all?" the lean dragon beside Nix suggested, his face twisted in confusion and awe as he looked to Vahly, then to his leader. He gestured toward the smoking ram with a hand that was missing two fingers. His youthful eyes and oddly aged face crinkled.

"Shut it, Roke," Baz snapped at the dragon.

He paced around the fist shape in the dirt.

With a quick hand, Nix helped Vahly to stand.

"I don't care if you are the supposed Earth Queen, human," Baz spat. "A bump in the ground isn't going to save anyone. We've already made our decision regarding the rising seas."

"Aye," Luc said. "We know death comes for us. It comes quickly. And we only wish to enjoy life's pleasures until that day arrives. If you can promise us gold..." His eyes shone like wet stones.

Baz sucked a breath and stepped closer. "Three full bags, and I'll consider keeping my rogues from bringing death to you immediately, and you too can enjoy the last of our days in this world."

So Luc and Baz were indeed both bingers. Perfect.

"I can manage three full bags," Nix said quietly. "But it'll take me one cycle of the moon to get it to you. And if I fail, find me at the cider house, and I'll submit to your payment in flesh and wing."

Vahly's stomach turned.

"You truly believe you can put your talons on that much gold in one moon cycle?" Baz rubbed his hands together, a binger's gleam in his eye.

"She can and she will," Vahly said, keeping her voice casual, confident.

Another male, this one with sea-green scales and ashen wings, turned away, toward the place where Vahly had killed their fellow. "Fedon?"

Vahly's throat seized and she glanced to Nix, who had paled. Fedon had to be the dragon that Vahly had killed.

The sea-green male looked at Baz. "You don't think

Fedon tangled with that mountain lion, do you? I'm going to check on him."

Sweat trickling down her temples, Vahly rushed to tug on the sea-green male's wing. "Eh, don't want to miss supper, do you? We have a great deal to discuss, and if I know dragons, there will be a lot of eating during the chat."

The young one named Roke raised his good hand. Vahly squinted through the fire's smoke as it drifted over the dragon.

"Aye, Tadeo," Roke said to the sea-green dragon. "I even found an egg to add to our feast!"

No! Vahly gasped, then coughed to cover the agonized sound. She rallied her wits, recalling the plan as she glimpsed Arc at the edge of the turn in the pass.

I could run in and reclaim your familiar, Arc said inside her mind. *Then you and Nix could flee. I doubt they could catch us. Not immediately, anyway. Do you want to alter the plan?*

No. I still have to explore the ruins. We must make peace somehow. I can't have dragons running around, ruining everything. This is such a mess. They're going to discover the body, and they'll know I killed him after seeing my magic.

"That is a gryphon egg." Vahly swallowed, her throat burning. Sweat dripped down her neck. "And we just happen to know a youngling at the Jades' palace who is keen on rarities such as that."

Nix snatched the egg from Roke's grasp. "I know the one you speak of, Vahly, darling." She raised an eyebrow at Baz. "He has a noble father who owns all the looms in the Jade territory these days."

"Druso? I know of him," Luc said, his voice gruff. "Not

an easy dragon. But he did have a male youngling on the way the day I broke the Call."

"If you want five bags of gold," Nix said, "allow us sell him this gryphon egg and rest and dine with you all this evening. It'll be perfect."

"Five bags." Baz's stern features smoothed. "Aye. Agreed."

I assume we'll further inebriate these rogues, make the first dragon's death appear to be an accident by way of rockfall or some such, then take our leave before sunrise?

Arc's voice danced inside Vahly's head. The pain began to recede as Nix tucked the egg safely into her own pack.

I am already mixing a potent beverage made of gold dust, air magic for fermentation, and these salt cedar blooms, Arc added. *This concoction actually smells rather tempting. I'll set the wineskin near the spot where you climbed the boulder, beneath the plank grasses. You can act as though you left it there for a future occasion.*

Vahly grinned. *You are beautiful, Arc. That's perfect.*

You find alchemists attractive? Is that a human trait?

She knew he didn't mean to sting her with a comment that would remind her that she was the last of her kynd. He was only curious.

Oh, yes. Alchemists were the best of companions, from what I've read in the dragons' scrolls about my kynd. Always making gold and better drinks. Quite alluring. Well, when they didn't smell of frog dust or eye of bat.

Arc's laugh whisked through her head. *I'll endeavor to remain pleasantly scented, then.*

Nix was chatting up Baz and Luc about the sharkstone smuggling job when she paused and turned her head, as if to listen. Vahly guessed Arc was filling her in on his concoction and possible ideas on how to proceed.

Vahly's magic pushed inside her chest like invisible hands pressing her heart and speeding the rush of blood through her veins. Her magic demanded that she claim the egg and go. But she forced herself to fetch Arc's powerful beverage, pass it around to the rogues, and sing four tavern songs as the dragons dropped, one by one, into a drunken sleep.

Then it was time to move the body.

Vahly winced, thinking of the grim duty. Pleasant evenings never started with corpses. Especially when said dead creature had fully armed dragon allies nearby.

CHAPTER THIRTEEN

Vahly, Arc, and Nix slipped away from the rogues and into the darkness.

The rise of dirt covering the rogue whom the others had called Fedon looked disturbingly similar to the mounds in which Mattin, former King of the Elves, had buried Dramour, Ibai, and Kemen, as well as Arc's friends, Rigel's son Pegasi, the ancient mother Vega, and the warrior Leporis.

Nix's amethyst-sapphire wings shivered in the moonlight. "If we can shift his grave closer to that old rockfall there, that would at least get him off the main game trail."

Vahly wiped beads of sweat from her upper lip. After eating and refraining from doing magic all evening, she did feel stronger. But not nearly as powerful as she had when she'd attacked Fedon. "I'll try to move the earth around him. You two might be forced to cart me back to camp though. I'm about done in."

Arc rubbed his hands together in excited alchemist

mode. She couldn't help but grin despite the situation at hand.

"Do you mind if I combine my magic with yours," he said, "and see if we can create a fresh fall of rock to mask the body?"

Nix looked over her wings, back toward the rogues. "Don't make too much noise or bring the mountain down on us all."

"I'm definitely not up to doing much." Vahly pressed her palms into the earthen tomb. The cool dirt was heaped head-high. This would be no easy task.

"You two will eventually shake the earth. I can tell that much," Nix said, throwing a wry grin at Arc.

Not making eye contact, Arc smiled—a private sort of grin that stirred a heat inside Vahly and made her wonder what he was imagining. If they hadn't been standing in the spot where she had been forced to kill a dragon, she would've raised an eyebrow and given him a line or two about what she thought. But sadly, it was quiet here, the air heavy with their knowledge of how much blood would have to be spilled in the coming days.

Arc looked down at his hands to weave golden strands of magic around his long fingers and double-jointed thumbs. Air magic lifted the ends of his hair, and the sound of wind rustling leaves grew loud even though there weren't many trees around. It was as if the Forest of Illumahrah whispered across the clearing in response to one of its royal masters.

Vahly forced all her energy into the Blackwater mark on her forehead and the drumming inside her palms.

Move, she ordered the earth.

The magic flowed from her in quiet, thundering waves, then combined with the sparkling breeze of Arc's power. With a rumble, the earth shifted the buried dragon and mounded against a tumble of large stones near the rock wall of the clearing.

Nix flew to the top of the rock wall and pointed to a spot. The moon glowed through her semi-transparent wings as she hovered, her flame-bright eyes blinking and her clothing fluttering in the wind that Arc's magic wrought.

Vahly and Arc traded a look, then focused their energy on the place Nix had selected.

The ground began to shake.

Nix turned in the air, watching the rogues' camp for movement, as stones began to tremble, then clack noisily on their way down the side of the rock face.

Nix held out both hands, her talons spread wide as if she meant for them to stop the rockslide.

Heart beating in her temples and palms, Vahly eased off the flow of earth magic. She dropped her hands at the same moment that Arc let his magic fall away.

A pile of rocks the size of Mattin's lapis lazuli bowl now lay atop the buried Fedon.

Arc came close, and Vahly leaned on him, beyond any fear of looking weak. He gave her a glass vial, wrapped in leather and corked. "Drink this," he said.

Nix landed beside them, her gaze shifting nervously.

Vahly took Arc's offered vial and downed its bitter contents. Her tongue shriveled at the taste, and she washed the potion down with a swig from Nix's water skin. Nix took off to fly one more time around the clearing while Arc helped Vahly to a mossy stretch out of sight from the trail.

A shaky breath gusted from Vahly. The egg sat safely in Nix's bag, propped against Vahly's knee.

"Your magic helped," she said to Arc.

"Did it? I think you accomplished the majority of that feat on your own."

"You're too kind, you know that? Quick. Say something horrible so I know you're not a figment of my exhausted mind."

"If Nix weren't here, and we weren't...in this sad situation, I'd be requesting an experiment on how it feels to kiss you in a windstorm of my making."

Arc's coal-black eyes studied her chin and throat. She could almost feel the drag of his gaze like fingertips over skin. The heat from earlier, the longing stirred by his grin, flickered again, stronger this time. Mountain mint and sun-warmed sap—Arc's scent—cocooned her and brought a dizziness far more delightful than the one that fatigue had rained down on her. Her head fell against his shoulder, and the intoxicating presence of his royal elven blood infused her like a balm, like wine, like the adventure for which she had always longed.

"Vahly. My queen." Arc's voice rubbed against her ears, strong and rolling like the sound of an earthblood vent just under the surface.

Shivers danced their way down Vahly's arms. She pressed her back against his chest, and he wrapped his arms around her, the muscles in his arms moving against her own. Her body lit up like a torch. Her breath came too quickly.

So this was what the desire to mate felt like.

Swallowing, she tried to breathe evenly, fighting the urge to spin around in the circle of his arms and throw herself on him like a fool.

"We should, maybe, we should get back to our camp before the rogues wake," she said, not recognizing her voice.

Arc stood and took her hand. "You're probably right, although I reserve the right to grumble about it." Vahly felt like she'd just leapt down from a tree limb, her stomach lifting and dancing. Arc winked, making Vahly bite her lip, then he turned his face to the moon. "Nix?" he called out quietly.

Nix flew overhead, her shadow interrupting the moonlight. She waved to them as Vahly shouldered her pack and tried to stop thinking about Arc's hands and mouth.

They crept around the sleeping rogues, holding their breath, Nix flying softly through the air and Vahly attempting to walk as quietly as Arc.

The path tripped Vahly twice on their way back to their own camp in the cave by the sea. Clouds covered the moon, darkening the trail. But despite the small struggles, they had fled with everyone fully intact. Experience had taught Vahly that situations rarely traveled the simple, comfortable path.

She didn't trust it.

"That escape was too easy," she said, thinking aloud now.

Nix landed and walked beside them as they rounded a grove of holm oaks. "Agreed. We'll have to keep a good eye out for those louts. They won't like us leaving while they slept. We took their egg and left nothing in its place. A promise of gold with no heart oath won't be enough to satisfy that Baz fellow for long."

"I do wish we didn't have to wait on Amona's warriors before heading into the ocean," Arc said.

The salty wind blew his surcoat around his powerful legs before whipping Vahly's hair into her eyes. The air stung her cheeks as she studied the lines of his back and shoulders. Her mouth was still dry from their shared moment near the rogues' camp.

"I don't love it," Vahly said, attempting to shake off the longing she felt for Arc's touch. "But the sea folk are more of a worry than avoiding rogues. If we can't handle a group of difficult dragons, what chance do we have against Queen Astraea?"

"But Astraea doesn't know you're headed into Bihotzetik," Nix said. Her stomach grumbled. "The rogues are fully aware we are in the area and ripe for whatever sadly unimaginative trouble they wish to start up. The enemy you know... and all that."

"What if she *does* know? After all, she had contact with Mattin. She has an insider somewhere in Illumahrah."

Arc halted and twisted, the focus of his gaze drawing the shape of her forehead, cheeks, and chin. "You don't believe it was only Mattin and Canopus? You think there is another elf working dark magic in the wood?"

"There's a chance," Vahly said.

Nodding, Arc continued walking. "I hope Cassiopeia keeps her wits about her."

"I don't think you need to fret on that beautiful beast's

account," Nix said. "That female has a head for ruling. She wears a crown of magic like it was crafted just for her."

"She's a wonder. It seems I am surrounded by wondrous females." Arc's lips tipped up at the edges as he grinned toward Vahly.

"I'm starving," Nix said, her stomach rumbling again to prove her point.

"When *aren't* you hungry?" Vahly elbowed her.

Nix raised her chin and narrowed her eyes at Vahly. "When you take a dragon into the wilderness and have her on guard duty twenty-four hours of the day, she's bound to need extra meals. Besides, there aren't any earthblood vents here. I have to get my energy from somewhere." She smoothed her red hair, and Vahly wondered how she managed to remain so sleek and beautiful in this wilderness she obviously loathed. "Anyway," Nix added, "I'm off to hunt. I'll return in an hour or so."

"Do you want us to come with you?" Arc touched one of his throwing knives.

Nix took off, then hovered above them. "Oh, no. You have your own hunting to do down here." She flew into the sky, stars showing between the racing clouds and her widespread wings.

Vahly's cheeks warmed, knowing quite well what Nix was referring to. She spoke to Arc without looking back at him. "Should I make you hunt me?" She fought a grin. "Or can we skip all that nonsense?"

When she turned around, his eyes had become those of a powerful elven royal. Goosebumps dusted over her skin. How was he interested in her instead of one of the gorgeous elves who lived in his homeland?

"There are times for nonsense, my queen," he whispered, his tone tempting.

Vahly swallowed, her body warming and her pulse like thunder. "Well, the rogues will sleep until the dawn. And we have to wait on Amona's fighters anyway."

Arc brought an orb of light to life in one hand. "Then come with me."

His words almost held the tone of command, but Vahly was certain it was only his royal blood strengthening the timbre.

"You don't have to ask me twice."

She walked with him to the cave where akoli vines choked the entrance, wild grapes glistening in a mirrored image of the stars. Arc pushed the vines aside and led Vahly inside.

Darkness poured over them as the vines resumed their guard duty at the cave's opening, but Arc's glowing sphere cast a golden net of illumination over the space. He released it to float on the gentle air of the cave. Vahly's heart kicked like a spring-crazed deer as she removed Nix's bag, tucking the egg against the wall.

After lowering her sword belt to the ground, she stood, pulse skipping, to face Arcturus. He'd removed his own pack and his knives too. They glittered in a neat pile on the other side of the shelter.

Arc took Vahly's face into his large, smooth hands, cradling her cheeks and chin. His breath was warm and his mouth so, so close. She touched the tips of his pointed ears, eliciting a sigh from him. He brushed lips over her forehead, warming her skin and sending tingling sparks of pleasure down her sides.

Lowering his chin, he met her gaze. His eyes reflected the orb's light, and magic twisted beside his temples in shades of twilight, starshine, and sunrise. He almost kissed her, stopping short.

"You have entranced me, Earth Queen."

"Is that so difficult to believe?" she teased.

Arc's arms encircled her. "You're alluring. Strong. Brave. Loyal. Humble. But the norm in times past is for the human to be infatuated with my kynd, not the other way around."

"Oh, don't you fret. I'm disturbingly infatuated with you."

His eyebrow lifted. "Disturbingly?"

"Well, at this point you could magick me right off the sea cliffs if I break your heart."

"Soon you'll be fully capable of annihilating me," he said. "Does that put you more at ease with this infatuation?"

"It does, actually. Revenge is sweet, elf. So watch yourself."

A twinge of alarm slid through Vahly's mind. Not her own feeling, but someone else's.

Amona.

Vahly. Daughter, we are nearly there. What is your status?

Amona herself was coming?

Vahly put her hands on Arc's broad chest. "Amona is talking to me." She tapped her temple. "They're almost here."

Arc's eyes widened. "She's early."

Wincing, Vahly left the warmth of his arms to gather her pack, even though half of her really wanted to stay in this cave, alone with Arc. But it couldn't be helped. When the dragons arrived, she'd have to immediately take the opportunity to swim into Bihotzetik. She couldn't lie around here with her handsome elven royal when the rogues might further complicate this quest at any moment.

"Yes," she said, gripping her satchel's rough strap. She would leave her sword and bow here. They'd be no use in the ocean. "A full day early unless you fogged my brain past working."

He laughed, and she heard him shuffling around beyond the light of the orb, gathering his things.

"Are you bringing your knives? I don't think I can do much with a short sword in the water."

"I think knives might prove useful. Do you want to carry one of them?"

"No, I think I'll have enough going on just trying to keep up with your swimming. You're bound to be better at it than me, being an elf and all."

At the mouth of the cave, he looked at her and ran a thumb along the side of her hand briefly, sending sparks burning down the underside of her arm. His eyes held mischief. The ocean wind tugged at his hair and the summer-scented vines around them.

"We simply must survive the sea now," he said. "I can't possibly give up the chance to properly kiss a human. What a wealth of scientific information it will provide!"

She punched him in the stomach and pretended it didn't hurt her hand. "Shut it, elf." Walking off, she teased him over her shoulder. "Revenge, remember? I might just become ridiculously powerful after our little swim. I'd be careful around me if I were you."

A flurry of beating wings sounded in the sky. Two sacks of clothing and weapons slammed to the grassy earth.

Vahly lifted a hand to block the rising sun's glare. They'd been up all night, but energy hummed through her body, excitement about discovering what her magic wanted her to find keeping her alert.

Amona and three other warriors—in full dragon form—descended on the coastline, their gazes bouncing between Arc, Vahly, and the vicious sea.

Ugh. Amona had brought Lord Maur. Xabier was the third, and he nodded his scaled head at her in greeting.

A distant wave crashed on dark rocks as Amona alone transformed out of her full dragon form, taking up one of the bags they'd brought and beginning to slide rings onto her fingers.

Because of course, rings were required in military operations. Vahly fought the urge to roll her eyes. Dragons.

When Amona had dressed, she approached Vahly, a genuine smile stretching her normally stern face. "Vahly, my daughter. I'm glad to see you well. Arcturus."

He bowed low. "Matriarch Amona, it is good to see you again."

"What has happened since we met last, Earth Queen? Any developments?" Amona asked.

Nix flew into sight, two deer in her talons. She threw the kill to the ground and greeted the dragons with a nod to each before Maur and Xabier began to tear the deer alongside her. Vahly wondered if they would save some for Amona, Arc, and herself. Nix threw a leg back and chomped it down. Vahly wasn't going to count on getting a portion.

"We ran into the rogues." Vahly's stomach turned in anticipation of diving into the ocean.

What would she find? Would her magic guide her? And would she somehow know if any sea folk were in the area? What if she got Arc killed in the process? She breathed out, trying to calm herself.

Arc handed his water skin to Amona, who accepted the offering and drank the entire contents down, not spilling a single drop. She dabbed her lips with the back of her lapis-lazuli-colored hand, then settled her gaze back on Vahly.

"What happened?" Amona asked.

Vahly filled her in on the tale of the egg and the killing she'd had to do. Amona hummed, impressed, as Vahly told her about raising the wall of earth and the second instance of Arc's magic combining with hers to create a greater effect. Amona glanced at Arc, a question in her features, but before she could run Arc through an impromptu power investigation, Vahly explained who Luc was and how their leader, Baz, seemed to be a true scoundrel. Amona scowled through the entire telling of the story but became downright indignant when Vahly told her the lie about selling the gryphon egg.

"If that tale finds its way to Eux, she will question the Lapis about you. Like me, she wants nothing to do with Call Breakers infiltrating her palace."

Vahly shrugged. "We had to tell them something to get the egg back."

"What is it about this egg that draws you so?" Amona asked.

Vahly took the egg from her satchel and handed it to

Amona, who turned the plum-spotted prize over in her hands gently.

"For a reason only my magic knows, the creature inside is family."

Amona's forehead wrinkled in thought, then she returned the egg to Vahly. "That must suffice for now, I suppose. But again, I don't want you to further tempt Matriarch Eux's temper. Who knows what kind of trouble she could cause, even if it would be to her own detriment? Jades don't think before they act, and well you know it, Daughter."

"I don't even know if the rogues believed us about anything. They might very well be hunting us right now."

"All the more reason for us to begin our adventure immediately," Arc said, his voice clear and respectful.

Amona led Vahly and Arc to the wild feasting. Two haunches of deer remained. Nix, Blackwater bless her, was roasting the meat with her own dragonfire. When it was burned at the edges, she shifted into her human-like form and dressed while Amona checked Xabier's right wing. He must have dinged it up in the rush to get here.

"Looks fine," Amona declared, sending Xabier back to his food.

"And your roasted portion is ready, Matriarch," Nix said to Amona before winking at Vahly. She knew when to kiss tail.

"Thank you." Amona clasped her ringed fingers. "As soon as Vahly and Arcturus are fed and ready, they will enter the sea."

Lord Maur grunted, still in his dragon form. He blew a burst of dragonfire toward the white-capped waves. For once, Vahly agreed with him. She didn't like the ocean any more than he did.

Xabier jerked his snout toward the northern headland. He must have been talking with Amona telepathically, because she answered aloud.

"Yes, Xabier. Please cover the spit of land there. Watch the western approach." Amona's eyes narrowed as she stared at the glassy, black surface of the sea. The wind had calmed, and the ocean grew eerily quiet.

"Lord Maur, you will fly over the southern approach, watching for unusual currents or anything that might resemble spellwork."

Maur bowed his head, then took off in a series of heavy flaps that blew Vahly's trousers and shirt against her body. Xabier followed suit and flew toward his assigned post.

"Nix, I believe it would be good for you to remain here, in the place where Vahly and Arcturus will come back out of the sea. To be certain their return is covered."

"Agreed." Nix left for the cave they'd been using as a home base, then returned in full dragon form.

Amona finished her meal. Her half-slitted eyes studied Arc while he gazed toward the ocean. It looked as though she was still deciding whether or not to trust him. "I'll fly a constant circle above the ruins themselves."

Vahly's stomach clenched. "Over the water? You don't need to do that. Please, stay on the coast unless I Call you."

"I did not ask for your permission, Daughter. You may be the Earth Queen, but I'm still your mother."

A grin flashed over Arc's mouth but was gone before Vahly could glare at him for it.

But no more time remained for arguing. Maur's and

Xabier's shapes were visible on the land that cradled the bay.

The sea awaited its foe, and Vahly could stall the confrontation with its salty depths no longer.

CHAPTER FOURTEEN

On the scarlet coral balcony of Álikos Castle, Queen Astraea blasted the report with a blinding white spell, and her protégé jerked in surprise. The lovely singer the queen had rescued from her abusive parents—Larisa—properly trailed Astraea, soaking in every decision and the persona the queen used in varying situations. But right now, Astraea was too infuriated to be pleased. Rippling eddies tossed the remains of the message that her scouts had scratched into the palm shell.

Still, none had seen Ryton.

He was swimming about the Bihotzetik ruins, chasing that Earth Queen, but apparently with no success, since they'd had no report.

"Will you tell me what is happening and what you will do for our kynd?" Larisa asked in her pearly voice.

"I'm wondering where my High General is and how he could possibly fail me. He is capable, vicious, practical.

Perfect for this type of thing." Astraea took one of her own necklaces and tied it around the singer's throat. Larisa's gills flared delicately as the white spheres settled below their slitted openings. "But maybe our General Ryton needs a touch of help?" Astraea locked gazes with Larisa, who was just a babe, the innocence still bright in her eyes. "I have kept something from you, and I should not have."

"Everything you do is exactly what must be done, my queen."

Astraea ate a handful of tideberries and paced, her dress sliding over the balcony's rails like golden eels. "Do you remember how late I was with General Venu and the scout Echo last night?" Usually, they had a pre-sleep discussion of the day's events, but Astraea had skipped it.

Larisa nodded.

"I sent my warriors to General Grystark's house."

"The one who questioned you about General Ryton?"

"The very same."

"Did you have him beaten? He deserved as much, my queen."

Astraea chuckled and opened her mouth to take in a cool current riding the tides around the castle. "Sometimes, such treatment makes them work to the best of their abilities. Other times, well, you must be more subtle. Tell me, singer. What do you fear more? The shark swimming before you or the shark hiding in wait?"

"The second."

"Exactly. A bit of unexpected behavior, a touch of cloaking... These techniques break your rival's stride, his rhythm. So much stronger than a mere strike to the face or back. One's fearful imagination puts all kinds of torture to shame." Astraea was pleased to see the singer smile.

Astraea whirled. "Bring Grystark to me at once," she barked at a servant.

"Yes, Queen Astraea."

Of course Ryton was suited to this task. His delay in completing this last step toward Astraea's final dominance over the entire world had to be due to some complication. Perhaps he needed someone to create a distraction for him?

The new elven queen—Cassiopeia, she was called—could be helping the Earth Queen. The spy had told her an elf of royal blood traveled at the Earth Queen's side, aiding her with his air magic.

So maybe it was time for the elves to have something more pressing to deal with?

Like the destruction of their entire plateau.

Astraea lifted the corner of her mouth as Grystark approached with a bow.

"You asked for me, my queen?" The general's graying hair and sharp eyes spoke of his experience. He was no Ryton—not nearly as loyal—but he would do the job well enough to distract the elves from giving the Earth Queen further aid.

Yes, that would do nicely.

Astraea would attack Illumahrah, then Ryton would return with human blood on his mighty hands. Desire pooled in the queen's heart. She would reward him well.

Astraea swam around Grystark in slow circles. He kept his head down because he knew what was good for him today. The general wasn't always so well behaved. She ran a finger along the edge of his spear, and garnet tendrils uncurled from a tiny cut as she smiled at the pain.

"How is your wife?"

Grystark's swallow was loud. "The healers believe she will live."

Astraea raised an eyebrow. "Do they? I heard the attack was incredibly vicious. And in the middle of the night, while you were both sleeping? And they took nothing?" She fought the urge to laugh at his shifting weight and the hate burning in his eyes. Ah, so he did know it had been on her orders. "What do you plan to do to prevent such unpleasantness in the future?"

Raising his head, he stared beyond her, unseeing, rage tightening his aged features. "My only goal in my life is but to serve you, my queen."

Cocking her head, she smiled at him. "Very good. Because I have an assignment for you and for all the armies. A true test of what we can accomplish."

Grystark blinked. "But General Ryton is away, Your Majesty."

"All the better for a test in case he is injured or taken down in battle. Today, our forces will mount a full attack on the Forest of Illumahrah."

The general nodded his head obediently. The queen wondered if he was picturing his wife's blood and the jagged length of coral that had speared her chest last night.

"I'll call up the units. Will you lead us?" Grystark's voice was flat.

"Yes. You are dismissed." She turned to yet another pathetic, whimpering servant. The thing was shaking like a tailless minnow. Her hand cracked across the servant's cheek. "Grow a spine and fetch my armor. Today, we will destroy an entire race of enemies."

Taking up her spear, Queen Astraea grinned.

Everything was going swimmingly.

CHAPTER FIFTEEN

V ahly stood still as Arc used his royal elven blood to paint a circle on each of her temples and one down her nose. He drew a line of his blood across her collarbone. Her lungs reacted immediately, and she took the most satisfying deep breath of her life.

"Not bad, elf. I wonder what kind of magic I'd be able to do if I shoved your spleen up my nose."

"Perhaps it would filter out foul odors." Arc's lips twitched.

"That would be such a blessing at the cider house during the winter when Nix keeps the doors shut."

Arc took up the paste he'd made of the eyewort and smoothed it over Vahly's closed lids.

"I'm guessing I look like some mysterious creature from another time." Vahly wiggled her eyebrows.

A band of sticky plant juice ran across her eyelids and the bridge of her nose. She could feel Arc's blood tingling under her skin, the magic spreading through her body. She had to admit to herself that she liked the idea of his power in her blood and bones. The thought of his power with spellwork and his air element breathing through her, well, it made her breathless in more than one way.

She swallowed and forced herself to look away from the ferocity in his black eyes and the defined edges of his cheekbones. He was cleaning his hands in the grass and whispering spells in the elven tongue, his full lips moving quickly.

Amona had flown one complete circle above the ruins. She landed and spoke into Vahly's mind. *Are you prepared, Daughter?*

I'm covered in elf blood and plant guts.

Is that a Yes?

I suppose in this instance it is.

Amona's lip curled into what might have been a smile had she been in her other form. She glanced at Arc, then took off, her wing beats blowing Vahly's hair back.

A THOUSAND FEARS ASSAULTED VAHLY AS SHE AND ARC maneuvered over the rocks toward the deep water.

Arc had said the magic would hold even if the sea washed the blood away. But the plant that was meant to help Vahly see wasn't magic. Though rare and new to her, it was obviously a simple healing arts paste. Surely the ocean would clean the mixture from her eyes and she would be lost, the watery world going blurry around her. And were those terrifying creatures with black fins and pointed teeth in this area? Even if she and Arc managed to evade sea folk, they could still be ripped to shreds by one of those enormous, carnivorous fish.

"My hair will be a disaster after all of this," Vahly joked, covering her fear.

"You are strong and your magic has led you to this. I'm confident we'll be successful." Arc jumped from the last of the coast's rocks into the water. Bobbing back to the surface, he looked up. His black hair clung to his head, highlighting the proud shape of his warrior's face. The small scar beside his nose. Tiny scratches along his jawline and cheekbones that made Vahly think of a bronze statue that had been roughly polished over a great span of time. His eyes showed the alchemist side—darting gaze, taking in information, always analyzing.

Vahly gathered her courage, and with one last glance at Nix on shore and Amona flying above, she dove into the water.

Arc submerged alongside her, gave her a once-over, then held out a hand.

Lead the way, my queen.

The ocean's filtered sunlight possessed the sky's hue and the pale jade of the seaweed growing far below. The water chilled Vahly's skin. Her linen shirt and trousers clung to her as she kicked and spread her arms wide, then pulled them back.

Shapes the color of charcoal, fog, and obsidian rose before them.

Vahly's heart surged.

Here it was. The ruins of the great city of Bihotzetik.

Arc's plant and blood magic seemed to be working. She could see clearly and breathe normally. A tentative smile slid over her mouth, her heart lifting, but the gnawing sensation in her stomach only grew stronger to overcome her struggling hope. Water extended for miles upon miles. This was very different from swimming in the Silver River. Of course, the salt water bit at her and there was the magic she had to have to function down here, but it was so much more than that.

At any moment, the sea folk could rush through the blurred and foreign world and kill her, also destroying any chance for Nix, Amona, and Arc to live a full, long life. The Sea Queen had made her declaration of war, her announcement that she and her army would smother the world in water. And there would be no changing her mind. Not after eons of feuding. Queen Astraea's vehemence for achieving ultimate power and control hadn't wavered.

Vahly had to survive this quest into the sea and make the risk they were all taking worthwhile.

The earth's heartbeat drummed dully here, its strength lessened by the water. But she could still hear it in her ears and feel it in her chest. Magic tugged at that one spot near her heart, telling her to push forward, to strive onward, to uncover whatever it was she needed to fully wake her powers and become a true Earth Queen.

Shops and homes with tiled roofs crowded in circles and along roads. The juxtaposition of a dwelling developed for ground travel set into this watery place made her head spin. It was disorienting to think that she was basically flying over a city that her ancestors had built.

A few strokes ahead of Arc, Vahly swam deeper into the city.

Every house boasted what she guessed was a sigil for

the family who had lived there. The house to her right showed a boar on a green field. Next door, the owners had used a hawk as their symbol. Across the street, three houses in a row showed the same sigil—a stag with a wide set of antlers.

They must have had a great many children, Arc said inside Vahly's head.

An invisible knife sliced through Vahly's chest. Human sisters. Brothers. A father and a mother. The sea folk had killed her mother during the flooding of the Lost Valley. Amona had told Vahly the tale.

Arc was looking through the window of the three stag-marked homes. Vahly swam inside, and Arc followed her. Wide shelves seemed to have served as beds for the humans. They were stacked one on top of the other by way of tree trunks. Vahly ran a hand over the long-submerged wood. The grain was coarse and slimy. Perhaps the salt water had somehow petrified the trunks, turning the wood to stone. Nothing was left of any blankets or pillows that might have been here during the city's life.

Barnacles and emerald sea moss covered the surface of the nearest bed. Vahly touched the spot where a head would have rested at night and wondered who had slept there.

Vahly assumed that her father had died the same day as her mother. That was logical. But what of her siblings? It was likely her mother and father had borne more children. What had they been like? Perhaps they'd slept in beds such as these, their heads turned so they could talk and joke late into the night. Had they been forced to watch as their mother saved Vahly on that fateful day and not them?

Vahly covered her ears, their imagined shrieks echoing in her mind, their faces twisted in horror as Amona lifted Vahly into the sky. What had their deaths been like?

Vahly. Arc gripped her arm, his solemn face coming into view and wiping her manic imaginings away. *Breathe. You're shaking badly. Do we need to go back? We can try again later. You may need time to absorb the intensity of the situation here.*

She took a breath, feeling like she'd been gored by a boar's tusk. *I'm fine,* she lied. *Let's keep going. Sorry for the dramatics.*

No apologies. This must be very difficult. I cannot imagine the pain in your heart at seeing this, at seeing what you lost.

Putting a fist against her churning stomach, Vahly pressed onward.

The tattered remains of a basket lay in a rough circle beside the last of the stacked beds. Several ruined scrolls sat inside. Fish had eaten away most of the vellum; the wooden rods of the scroll Vahly lifted crumbled into the water. The copper knobs that had been on the ends of the wooden rods sat in the mess on the floor, their metal green with age. She'd get no information from scrolls here.

With a nod to Arc, she swam out of the large home and into the wide avenue. A chill shook her as pale-bellied fish —as large as Xabier or Helena the healer in dragon form— drifted overhead like ghosts. She shivered. This was far more eerie than she'd thought it would be. She'd been so focused on following her magic that she hadn't considered the emotional impact this place would have on her.

Steeling herself and remembering her human mother's courage, she moved forward.

Beyond the houses, five shops with faded red walls

made a circle around a mosaic of smoky-gray and ivory tiles. The mosaic showed interlocking oak leaves and the face of a woman with a narrow jaw and full, pink lips. Was this an Earth Queen? Perhaps touching the image would somehow help her own magic rise...

But when her fingers brushed the tiles, no insight or vision materialized, no deep awareness. No hunch on what this person might mean to the history of who and what Vahly was. Sighing, she swam on.

The nearest shop stocked the remains of what must have been rugs. Only patches of the wool and cotton remained, strings of ruby, emerald, and onyx. Most of the color had gone gray from the salt water. Vahly swam around the shop.

A great black spire rose in the distance.

Energy rushed over Vahly's scalp and down to her chest. She grabbed Arc's arm. Earth magic drummed through her bones as if it wanted to speak to her.

As if the magic wanted to say, *Yes. There.*

Arc treaded water. *That's the first of the cathedral's spires.*

Why does one building need five spires?

They swam on together, bubbles rising from their mouths and dancing away from the city to the sunny surface of the water.

The five most powerful Earth Queens in history added a spire, Arc said.

Vahly felt like she'd been punched in the stomach. She paused, floating, unmoored. *They built that with their magic?* Stones. She'd never be able to do magic like that. Not a chance.

Arc eyed her like she was a puzzle he was trying to solve.

She frowned and swam on, wishing she didn't long for him to pipe up with another of his optimistic sentiments about Vahly being the one to bet on.

The first section of the massive cathedral rose from the sea floor. Like a spear thrust through the sand by an unknown god hiding inside the world's core. Vahly's reflection showed in its obsidian surface.

Earth magic pulsed through her blood and bones three times.

A hand knocking on a door. Rap. Rap. Rap.

This was exactly where her magic wanted her to be.

The building stood straight and true, like smooth tree trunks banded together by an invisible force. The structure's distant, tapering peak foamed the surface of the water, curling pearly clouds of ocean around its tip. A school of bottle-nosed fish—Vahly thought perhaps they were called dolphins—glided past the upper reaches of this spire. Their tails flashed the inconsistent sunlight against the cathedral's glossy exterior.

Not bad, Vahly said.

Indeed. Arc placed a hand on the cathedral, his eyes narrowing on the stone. *It's obsidian.*

Fast-cooled molten rock? That's what I had guessed.

Yes. The Earth Queens raised the lava so quickly that it remained smooth as it formed under their command. The rock material is unable to form its usual crystalline structure because of the speed of the magic.

A sudden current rushed between them, pulling at

clothing and hair. Vahly looked over her shoulder, but the city slept as it had for generations despite the strange and powerful eddy. The water yanked Arc's shirt against his body, and his collarbone showed like a blade in a beam of sunlight. He kicked his legs like he'd been born to swim, steady and sure. Vahly felt like she was thrashing just to stay put.

You sure you don't have a touch of sea folk in your blood? Vahly raised an eyebrow at him before swimming into the cathedral's door.

She would've been sweating if she hadn't been underwater. That current was a keen reminder that sea folk could attack at any moment. They had to stay alert. She had to keep from being too consumed by this cathedral and what it might mean for her future as Earth Queen. If she was distracted and the sea folk arrived, she was as good as dead.

A ten-foot tall opening led to a cavernous room, whose gold-painted ceilings were nearly too far away to see. Mosaics set with tiny tiles of vermilion, smoke, amber, and verdigris covered every inch of the walls. Long benches lined the floor, some fallen and eaten by the salt water, others intact as if Vahly's kynd had just stood up and walked out of the cathedral not two minutes ago. Her stomach clenched with a longing that was an echo of the feeling she'd had at the bridge with the Spirit of the River.

This place must have flooded slowly for the benches to remain upright as they were. So strange. She tried to imagine the day everyone had died, and how the Earth Queen of the time would've fought against the water. There was no evidence of her battle around this spire. Perhaps signs of a fight would show themselves at the other sections of the cathedral.

Of course, the previous Earth Queen had been very weak. Vahly was almost certain she hadn't added a spire, because the former King of the Elves, Mattin, had tricked both her and her predecessors with the diluted Blackwater. The loss of direct interaction with Blackwater over the generations had resulted in that last Earth Queen being completely unable to defend her people from the sea folk.

Vahly said a silent prayer. Hopefully, her own powers would rise strong and capable. But her own magic had come from her ancestors. Mattin's generations-long trickery would surely have an adverse effect on Vahly too.

She allowed herself to drift toward the front of this section of the cathedral. If the other four areas were as awe-inspiring and detailed as this one, searching for what her magic wanted her to find would take an eon. So far, her magic had only knocked hard that first time. She assumed that meant she had not yet stumbled onto the truth it wished to reveal. Of course, she could be completely wrong.

A hulking table lorded over the front of the room, fashioned from an oak's trunk that the humans had cut across and left in a rough-hewn state. A multitude of lines showed the age of the cut tree at around four hundred and fifty years, by Vahly's approximation.

Another rush of water made Vahly glance over her shoulder, her nerves jumping. But Arc treaded water at the door. He was on watch and didn't look alarmed, so she continued searching through the altar's treasures.

A bronze candelabrum lay on its side, so Vahly set it straight. The candles were long gone, but the flame-snuffer endured, its patina green and the hinge stiff. A tiny trunk reminded Vahly of Nix's money box back at the cider house. On this chest, circular lapis lazuli stones threaded in thick bands of pyrite decorated the top and sides. A gem like a multi-faceted raindrop glittered near the latch. The latch's stone had obviously been cut to refract light and did its job well.

Vahly longed to keep it. The old Vahly would have used it to play Trap with the high rollers at the cider house, but today's Vahly had no time for that kind of gambling.

Unfortunately, she was forced to gamble with her life, as well as everyone else's.

Shaking her head, she placed the small trunk beside the candelabrum, then headed toward the back wall of the room.

An algae-cloaked mosaic covered the wall, and with one look, Vahly felt magic pounding through her heart.

She bent double, the tug of her power almost painful.

Vahly? Arc swam to the side of the door, glancing back and forth between her and the exit.

She straightened and paddled disjointedly behind the oaken altar table to get a better look. *I'm all right,* she said, even though she wasn't so certain.

A swathe of lime-colored algae veiled the artwork, but she could tell darker and lighter tiles did indeed make up an image. An image her magic demanded she see in full.

I assume you have found something of note, Arc said.

Using her forearm, Vahly wiped the algae away. Frustrated that she couldn't move more easily in the water, she swam backward as quickly as she could in order to view the mosaic in its entirety.

It was a gryphon.

Her heart leapt three times, and a frisson of power electrified her blood.

The Bihotzetik people had arranged countless garnet tiles to form a gryphon. The creature's eagle wings stretched wide within a tangle of riotous forest growth— grape vines, oak leaves, and olive branches—and his lion paws clawed into a field of midnight earth and glittering stones.

The thrill of power steadied itself into a slow rhythm that buzzed through Vahly, head to toe.

This was definitely a part of what she needed to discover here in the sunken ruins of the former capital.

If you hadn't already told me that the egg was that of a gryphon, I'd know now. She turned to see if Arc was looking at the mosaic.

Arc smiled at the artwork. *Beautiful. So this trip into the sea is tied to what that unborn gryphon will mean for you.*

For us.

Each of the mosaic's four corners boasted a new scene. The top left showed a circle of jet black touched with diminutive tiles in the same glittering stones as the ones at the gryphon's feet. The Blackwater.

Vahly swam up to look closer at the circle. It was lapis lazuli. *It's Mattin's bowl. This is the Blackwater.*

Arc slipped through the water to the scene on the top right edge. He ran a broad hand over a gathering of animals. *This looks like a cliff owl and a bear. And here is a —*

A rock lizard and a dawn hawk. These are their animals. The

143

humans' animals. But what was this mosaic's point? Why was the gryphon in the center of these four scenes?

The corner below the Blackwater showed a bundle of cloth and pair of antlers. Vahly frowned, unsure what it could be. Engraved words ringed the two images, but the salt water had eaten the interior color away; the phrases weren't legible.

Can you read this somehow? she asked Arc. Perhaps his elven sight could pick up more than her human eyes.

Arc swam down, then cocked his head, studying the lines. His fingers moved over the image. *I'm not certain about the first part here, but the remainder is a spell. The words, they move me.* He made a fist and pressed it against his chest.

Vahly swam closer and brushed a palm over the spell. Her head felt light as a feather. *My magic agrees with you.*

Arc tapped his bottom lip with his thumb, his feet kicking to stay in place. *The section I can read says,*

'Two to twine,

Born to bind.

Earthen bred,

Power bled,

Alone alive' —*I'm not entirely sure about this part either* —*'as one to rise.' That is my best guess, anyway,* Arc said.

Born. Ah. So the bundle was a human baby. Perhaps the antlers indicated an animal familiar. Were they bound at birth? Or was this simply a reference to birth in another way?

The fourth corner of the mosaic held a sprawling oak. Vahly and Arc rubbed the artwork until the algae gave way to the tree's great limbs and roots, both of which were wider and more twisting than a dragon's tail, if the owls in the image were indicative of scale. The tiles that made up the earth at the base of the oak sparkled like coins.

It was so lovely, and the sight of it all lessened her terror of being down here under the sea. Her magic drummed a steady rhythm, and hope beamed inside her heart.

Then a sickening sound like a thousand breaking waves roared around them.

Vahly and Arc whirled to find the source of the noise.

A dark shape flew through the cathedral door.

It was one of the sea folk.

Feeling as though her chest were caving in, Vahly opened her mouth to scream as the sea kynd slammed Arc into the mosaic. Algae exploded in great clouds of emerald, and Vahly's hand went to where her sword normally hung, but of course, it wasn't there.

The clouds cleared even as Arc fought back with a cascade of inky, gurgling darkness that reeled the sea kynd around and pitched him backward. The sea kynd raised a scarlet coral spear, and the water—still twilight-hued from air magic—heaved in on itself. The current rushed at Arc in a torrent of whitewater. Arc's and the sea kynd's movements blurred with the twist and roll of the ocean. The sea kynd drove Arc across the room to smash into the cathedral's obsidian bones.

Vahly nearly felt the hit herself, her head throbbing and her vision clouding.

The sea kynd faced her.

For a moment, they both paused, the beat before the fight. A strange calm overtook Vahly as the currents tangled the sea kynd's ruddy beard.

Then he took off, aiming straight at her, his finned, powerful limbs driving through the sea, his eyes coal-hot, and a spear in his murderous hand.

Pulse roaring in her ears, desperate to access the earth and whatever sliver of power she might use against this vicious creature, Vahly shot toward the ground.

CHAPTER SIXTEEN

R yton had been patrolling the city, hiding among its shadowy structures and crumbling roads. He'd avoided the cathedral and its spires. The place reeked of earth magic and set his teeth on edge.

But then he scented her. The Earth Queen.

Raging through the water, he raced along the trail, nostrils and gills flaring. He whispered spellwork into his shell spear. Water magic gurgled and roared all around him, steadying him against the unholy thrum of the creature attached to his spine, the monster that would allow him to hunt the Earth Queen on land. The sickness of the being's foul power pulled at his energy. It was impossible how it both drove and drained him. He felt like he'd swallowed poison every day he'd risen with that thing on his back.

Blasting through the door, he barreled into the royal-blooded elf and raised his spear, pointing it ahead. All in a matter of seconds, the elf tried to grab Ryton with a powerful twist of air magic thrown into the currents. His magic overpowered the elf's, and the elf hit the wall. His body drifted, unconscious, as Ryton shot through the water toward the painted face of the Earth Queen. What magic was this that allowed her to breathe under water?

Triumph soaring through his soul, Ryton struck the female across the head with his spear. Blood spooled from the wound, but she did not falter as he would have guessed. She turned to him, eyes blazing with righteous fury, gripped the edge of a table, and shouted into the water.

The table exploded into a thousand pieces and flung themselves at Ryton like arrows.

Shocked, he was slow to react. The first of them pierced his flesh, but he felt no pain. He lifted his spear and shouted his own spell. His magic drove the jagged points of wood away from him and back at her.

Ryton blinked, unsure about what he was seeing. The wooden projectiles did not lance into her body. The wood veered around her as if it knew its mistress well.

But this was Ryton's world, here in the jeweled depths of the sea. And he knew exactly how to vanquish this queen.

His spear cut through the water, speeding in a blur of pale shell. Water swirled around him and the Earth Queen. The spellwork threw her to the ceiling of the cathedral. Her body hit the sloping, golden reaches and slammed hard, arms and legs going limp.

Grinning, Ryton swam after her, to finish her.

Before he could cast another spell, the Earth Queen's eyes flashed open.

She smiled, set her hands on the ceiling and spoke.

"Break." Her voice echoed, the dragon language sliding from her lips, a curse, a horror to Ryton's ears.

The cathedral opened up, cracking along the stone seams of the vaulted ceiling.

The Earth Queen swam up and away, Ryton following and quickly catching up.

Something hit him from behind. He whirled to see the elf, conscious again. Bruise-hued shadows poured from his fingertips like squid ink to surround Ryton, blinding him more thoroughly than any night could. He bellowed and struck into the dark with his spear and spells. The inky clouds drew away and he turned and twisted, searching for her. For him.

But they were gone.

He looked up, rage and frustration crawling up his neck, seething inside the black creature on his back, making him shake.

Across the rippling surface of the water, high above, the shadow of two dragons blocked the sunlight. Ryton swam hard. His mind tripped over what he was seeing. Were the dragons trying to rescue the human and the elf?

He knew the human had been raised by them. But to see the loyalty, the kinship, the risk the dragons took to save her in front of his eyes? Ryton could hardly focus on his mission.

The larger dragon lifted the elf free of the ocean.

Ryton closed the distance. His spear glanced across the Earth Queen's bare foot, and his spellwork sent a wave clawing up to grab her. The sea clamored around Ryton, lifting him toward the dragon that carried the Earth Queen.

The gurgling hands of salt water spilled over the dragon's legs and drenched the Earth Queen in full.

Fury defined her features as she screamed. The dragon shrieked, and his grip loosened. The Earth Queen began to slip below the surface. Keening, the dragon closed his hold on her again and wheeled in wild circles toward the shore.

Temples throbbing, Ryton shouted another spell and raised his spear.

The growing wave crested with him at its peak, water bubbling at his elbows and around his legs. The air washed over his face, harsh and empty.

He could breathe above the water, he realized belatedly. The foul beast he wore was doing its job.

With his magic, he drove the crashing, spelled salt water onto the rocks, where it spilled him out fifty feet from the dragons, elf, and Earth Queen. Stumbling, falling, he sucked a panicked breath before his hands hit the ground. He hadn't meant to drive himself ashore. He'd been so unsteadied by the feeling of the air filling his lungs, by the bizarre solidity of that which normally felt far too insubstantial to support his weight.

A dragon screeched, tearing the thickened air with a sound that had teeth.

The world spun, and Ryton's stomach roiled as he worked his way to standing.

The Lapis matriarch lowered her corpse-blue head and flew at him.

A different sort of fire burned under Ryton's flesh. Oh, how he hated her. This foul beast had killed his sister, Selene. This raging menace had morphed Ryton into a desperate servant to revenge. This monster had shredded the heart of his family.

Dragonfire spouted from the matriarch's foul snout.

Ryton leapt toward the cliff, just past the rocky breakers, then the sea welcomed him home.

But the dragonfire plunged into the waves, chasing him. Blood red and glaring yellow, smelling of sulfur and death, the flames dragged across his back. Pain exploded over Ryton's skin, and he jerked, arms flailing. The cursed thing on his spine emitted a horrifying squeal. Ryton forced himself to swim deeper, where the dragonfire could not reach.

At last, the teal sea cocooned him, cooling the burns along his lower back and left arm. The black creature between his shoulder blades blessedly went silent. He didn't care if it had died.

Flipping, he looked to the surface.

Three dragons soared over the waves before disappearing from sight.

A distant dragon's groan of pain echoed through the water, and Ryton thrilled to hear the glorious sound.

CHAPTER SEVENTEEN

Vahly's lungs burned as hot as earthblood vents as she swam toward the surface.

That thing was right behind them.

Everything was moving too quickly to absorb. Arc broke through the waves, and Amona reached low to snatch him from the ocean. Xabier swooped down to clutch Vahly in his careful talons. They were going to escape. The sea kynd wasn't going to rip her and Arc to pieces. But she couldn't catch her breath. Her pulse galloped, uncontrollable, wild.

The water sprayed upward and a wave lifted high. Something viciously cold pricked her bare foot, and a scream erupted from her, fury riding its wake.

Why couldn't she wake her full powers now? What was the point of being Touched if she couldn't fight when it truly mattered?

Her face shook as she clenched her jaw and tried to bring whatever magic she might have to the surface even though she had no idea what to do while hanging from a dragon's talons.

A sudden wave battered her and Xabier.

He shrieked, and she slipped, heart freezing at the thought of falling. Turning, she tried to see what was happening, where everyone was, including the sea kynd, but it was all water and talons and blurring vision.

Xabier listed hard to the left. Vahly's stomach dropped, and she yelped, eyes burning, Arc's air magic and the plant salve's power waning. As they careened over the shoreline, Xabier's wing spasmed—the spelled salt water blackened it inch by horrible inch.

The ground rushed up to meet them. Vahly's head and lungs were on fire. She rolled to a stop and vomited water into the sandy dirt.

Xabier fell onto his side a few feet away. Arc was running to him, Nix landing on the other side of Xabier. Amona took off into the sky again, her enormous sapphire wings spreading wide and her cry of rage filling Vahly's buzzing ears.

She found her feet. "Mother, no!" The sea folk would take her. This one was powerful. A general perhaps. Only the higher ranked of the sea folk could raise a wave like that.

But then Vahly saw what Amona did. The sea kynd was on shore, standing like he belonged there just as they did.

Amona blew fire at him, and he dove off the sea cliff, cleverly avoiding the rocks.

Xabier's shrieks dissolved into a garbled moan, and Vahly hurried as best she could toward him. Arc had his hands on the dragon's side, pouring healing light and dark into his damaged wing. But Xabier's left leg was what drew Vahly's attention. She swallowed, nearly vomiting again.

The spelled salt water had eaten the flesh to the bone. Pale white glistened above the blackened, gnarled remains of Xabier's foot and talons.

Vahly's hands fisted and she fought a sob of frustration and grief and fear.

She reached down, slammed both palms onto the earth, and willed the ground to rise at the drop that led to the rocks in the shallow water. The earth obeyed and heaped upon itself, rolling and rising until it formed a wall to protect Xabier, Arc, and Nix from further attacks. It wouldn't shield them from a major wave, but it was all Vahly could manage.

Her knees buckled, and she dropped, vision going dark.

Nix's voice leaked into the strange dreams that held Vahly in the darkness. "I'm not too proud. I'll sit on the egg if you think it might help us burn them all down." Her words were unusually clipped, anger slicing through her normally sultry tone.

Vahly sat up, and the world went sideways. She was in their cave. The vines across the entrance blocked the bloody red of a sunset. Or maybe a sunrise?

Arc put a hand behind her back. His hair fell over one of his eyes, and he brushed it behind one pointed ear. "How do you feel?"

"Like I've been stepped on by someone who eats more than Nix."

"Impossible." Nix winked. But then her eyes grew serious. "If you need to go back to sleep, we can keep watch. Everything is quiet for now. We have your little friend here, safe and sound." She lifted the egg and patted it.

Vahly's heart thudded against her ribs, and she reached for the egg. It fit snugly in her lap. She took a deep breath and looked up, ready to hear the bad news. "How is Xabier?"

Arc's face fell. He glanced at Nix, who winced at Vahly's question. "Matriarch Amona and Lord Maur brought him home to the Lapis healer. I couldn't heal him. The wounds were substantial."

"He won't make it, Vahly." Nix swallowed and turned her gaze toward the ground.

Vahly's chest tightened. She shut her eyes against the knowledge. Good Xabier. Sacrificed for her. By the Blackwater, she would do every single thing she could to be worthy of it.

"I'm sorry," Nix said. "I know you liked that young male. He seemed like a good one. Another loss. Another day. I can't wait to burn them all down." She touched her necklace and whispered something to herself.

"Maybe Xabier will struggle through. We don't know for certain. How long have I been out?" Vahly asked, feeling lost.

"Just the day. It's nearly nightfall," Nix said.

Nix offered Vahly a length of the plant that tasted like bacon, but Vahly shook her head. She was too nauseated too eat. Arc brought her some water, and she forced down two swallows, knowing her body needed it. Her skin felt like a sand flat at high summer. She touched her face. Instead of feeling the leftovers from the vision plant and the blood magic, her fingers found her forehead and cheeks smooth.

"Arcturus wiped your face clean," Nix said.

Vahly smiled at him in thanks.

Nix stood and shook out her wings, knocking debris from the cave wall. "I'm going to hunt, so if you'd like to give her a proper all-over wash, Arcturus, you'll have the time."

A sly grin tipped Arc's lips up at one end. "I'd like nothing more, but I don't believe our queen is in the mood for such attentions."

Vahly barely heard them. Her mind was on Xabier. They hadn't been close, but still. She'd worked with him, lived near him, gone to his ceremony so recently. A breath shuddered out of her, and she set both palms on the gryphon egg.

"I'll go outside," Arc said, gathering his bow and quiver. "You need some time alone if I'm not mistaken."

"Thank you. For everything. You were amazing down there under the water. I would have died if it weren't for you and the clever use of your air magic."

He bowed gracefully, then looked up at her through thick, black lashes. "I live to serve you, my queen."

Vahly let her tears for yet another friend lost fall onto the gryphon egg. "I pray I don't have to lose you too."

Her hands shook, and she blinked, shocked at the battle, at the outcome of her venture into the sunken ruins. Yes, she'd seen four scenes that might somehow help her gain more power, but it was cased in riddles and had no clear meaning. And the sea kynd had come onto land! That... thing on his back had been a monstrosity. A bitter taste touched the back of her tongue. If he could come ashore, they would have to keep an even closer watch on their surroundings.

Her teeth ground together. Stones, how she hated the sea folk.

Poor Xabier. She couldn't even imagine how horrible it would be to lose more dragons to the ocean. To watch Amona's flesh blacken. To see Nix's wings dissolve into a mess of gore and bone. She'd have to see all the horror if her magic didn't wake in full. Her stomach clenched, and she gripped the egg more tightly, taking comfort from its presence.

Vahly's teardrops slid down the sides of the speckled egg and gathered in the space between the shell and Vahly's fingers, which were dirty from raising the earthen wall in her attempt to protect Xabier from further harm.

The salty moisture began to warm.

Vahly cocked her head, wondering if she was imagining the heat.

But the tears at the base of the egg, near her fingers, grew hotter. Too hot to hold, in fact. Sucking a breath, she set the egg on her pack, then blew on her reddened fingertips. She stared at the ivory, speckled oval, the treasure she'd been carrying for days on end.

The egg trembled.

Her breath caught.

A jagged crack split one side of the shell.

CHAPTER EIGHTEEN

Queen Astraea and her entire army—a whirling mass of scarlet coral spears and finned bodies—swam down deep to the blackest region of the sea, near the bedrock. The island's base appeared, a bone-white wall in the darkness. The arched entrance to Ryton's tunnel opened like the mouth of a whale, and Astraea charged inside, her warriors at her back.

She glanced at General Grystark, who rushed ahead to catch up to her. His ashen eyebrows furrowed, and his armless shoulder twitched as he swam. With his remaining hand, he raised his spear to salute her, then called up a spell to illuminate his weapon. The magicked spear cast enough light for the advance units to see inside the tunnel's black maw.

General Venu kicked his legs in a burst of speed and came up beside them. "My queen," he said, water bubbling at the ends of his eel-dark hair and around his mouth, "you're certain the tunnel is clear? The most recent engineers' report stated the last third of the passage remained unstable, and I humbly urge you to—"

"Do not question our queen, General Venu." Grystark stared straight ahead. A muscle at his jaw tensed.

Astraea smiled. Attacking Grystark's wife Lilia had been such a wise decision. Now, the general was truly at her beck and call. "Venu, do you not believe in risking all for the good of our kynd?"

Venu paled and dipped his chin respectfully. "Of course I do, my queen."

The tunnel veered southeast, then sank deeper. Venu illuminated his spear to join Grystark's, and soon the advance units followed suit. The army coursed through the tunnel that snaked beneath the island, water rushing along their steely faces and powerful limbs.

A plume of dust rained from above, and Astraea dodged a sinking rock that had fallen from the ceiling. Venu's gaze touched her for a moment, but her glare put him back on task.

Yes, there was risk here, and well Astraea knew it. But annihilating the elves who had turned on her, the elves who were now supporting the new Earth Queen, was key to accomplishing her ultimate goal of swaddling the entire world in water. Today, they would take out those arrogant, betraying, loathsome elves, and the Earth Queen would have one less army at her back. Then the Earth Queen would only have one army to support her—the dragons.

If Ryton failed to assassinate her, the war would continue on more even ground. Astraea with her one force and the Earth Queen with her scaly allies. The elves were a wildcard, unpredictable with that magic of theirs. She'd discounted their place as enemies for a long while, thinking them weak and unfit for fighting sea folk, but the Earth Queen had bothered to treat with them. There must have been a reason for her efforts, some power that Astraea had yet to see in the elves. They had to be eliminated.

A thundering echoed down the tunnel.

Astraea's heart skipped, her gaze tearing across their path, looking for the source. "What is it? Grystark, swim ahead!"

His eyes shuttered, then he plunged onward.

The warriors behind Astraea slowed. She spun and raised her voice, the sound trumpeting through the water with her sea kynd magic.

"Fear not! We own this day! Faster now! Faster!"

Mouths drawn and white knuckles on spear shafts, the advance units poured past Astraea to follow Grystark.

Then a rock ledge the size of Astraea's throne room broke from the tunnel's wall and collapsed on the warriors. The dusty stone trapped a dozen or more, and the sea folk behind Astraea shrieked.

Hissing, Astraea drew back from the billowing particles of broken rock, then swam onward, her temples pounding. "Don't be cowards! Keep on!"

Screams rippled through the eddies created by the fallen ledge.

As Astraea slipped through the cloudy water, over the fallen debris, a warrior reached a hand out for help. She kicked past. That fighter was already dead. There was no saving one crushed by such a fall.

Grystark swam out of the gloom, warriors zipping past him and heading onward. "My queen," he shouted, his voice tight as they swam forward again, "We must retreat. We've lost half a unit already."

Astraea's blood sizzled, and she struck out at Grystark with her spear. He reacted quickly, raising his own weapon, then rage swallowed Astraea whole. She shouted a spell that burned her throat with its intent, the warbling words meant to kill.

The spell shot Grystark, and his limbs froze in the water. Astraea let the others swim past, her gaze locked on her work. He deserved this and more. Traitor. Doubter. Unfaithful.

As Grystark's eyes grew hazy and fluttered closed, she nuzzled into his neck. "Your wife will die this night. Slowly. Surely. And her blood is on your hands."

Blood singing with victory, she shoved him away into the depths.

ASTRAEA AND THE REST OF THE ARMY EXPLODED FROM THE END of the tunnel into a sea painted in shades of sunrise. Headed away from the Lapis shoreline, they rushed toward Illumahrah, through a gusting southward current, speaking spells to fight the water's undertow. As ordered, the units encircled the peninsula that housed the ancient land forest.

Venu hurried to Astraea's side. "My queen! General Grystark is missing. I have taken control of his brigades."

"Then move ahead with the first strike."

The warriors Ryton had trained to multiply salt water gathered at the tip of the peninsula. The sounds of their spellwork crashed through the azure and pink world, a churning, smashing noise that was music to Astraea's ears.

They weren't as good as she was at the new magic, but they weren't bad. She grinned as the water built and rose above their heads. A great wave gathered, then Venu's folk jabbed their spears at the new salt water.

The storm of spelled liquid thundered at the peninsula.

Astraea dashed to the rough surface, breached, and called water to carry her closer. She didn't want to miss a moment.

Sliding two tympanic leaves over her gills, she rode her own small wave to the very edge of the shoreline. Venu and many others joined her.

The giant wave curled at its tip, frothing like a rabid beast before raging inland to rip castle-sized trees at the root and wash verdant greenery and black earth from its home.

"Are they all still asleep?" Astraea gripped her spear in both hands, face stretched with a vengeful smile. "I hope they show up to fight. I'd love to see what they can do."

But there was no sound from the elves. No outcry or shout for a defense. Salt water gushed over possibly half of the peninsula from what Astraea could see. Trees shook in the seething mass of water, their roots bobbing to the surface.

Astraea faced Venu. "Call for another great wave. I don't think we've reached the more populated areas."

Venu dove like a bolt of lightning, and before Astraea knew it, another enormous wave roiled into being. She applauded the power of the creation as the watery form steepled high. The wave punched into the Forest of Illumahrah, deep and far beyond the reach of the first strike.

Shouts reverberated across the water. Golden light erupted from the sparkling waves, and a wind born of air magic tossed Astraea's hair. An army of elves floated above a third great wave that Astraea's clever warriors had assertively called up.

"Now, this is interesting. Let us see what they do with this." She whispered a spell, her lips brushing the cold coral of her spear.

"Jagged, breaking,
Pulling, tugging,
Take them deep."

Her spells were not worded as prettily as Ryton's, but they were far stronger because of her Touched mark and the forceful capacity of the magic boiling in her veins.

A lone female elf with a swirling crown of light and dark leapt from one floating tree to another. Astraea couldn't see her clearly from this distance, but it was obvious this was the Queen of the Elves. Her sunlight-colored tresses flared around her face and her hands held storms of night and day.

The Elven Queen threw her magic at Astraea.

Wind tore the tympanic leaves from Astraea's gills and left her gasping. Blood racing, she dove into the water only to be tangled in a false night, the darkness swamping her senses entirely. She set her jaw, then swam directly toward the surface. That creature would not be the end of her. How dare the elf even attempt it?

Tearing out of the water and leaping high, Astraea eyed the elf. Some of the elven folk grasped for branches or logs that rolled and jostled in the tumult, while others were aloft like the Elven Queen, leaping from one pile of floating debris to another with impressive jumps. A male with bulging eyes shouted to the Elven Queen as he went down, and the Elven Queen risked a whipping lash of whitewater —a wave that could drag her under—to snag his arm and pull him to safety beside her.

Two of Astraea's warriors rose from the waves and aimed spinning columns of water at a group of magic-wielding elves. Light flashed around the elves, their gusts whirling the water away from their perch on a flat of wood. But the columns of water, their sound almost deafening, would end them.

The Elven Queen spread her arms wide, and a net of gold and inky darkness linked her hands. Making a sweeping motion, she appeared to fly through the air. She thrust herself between the spinning columns of water to protect the others. The columns blasted her, and she disappeared into crashing water.

"Gone so soon?" Astraea whispered, enjoying the show.

All around the area, elves battled her warriors with light orbs and unspooling purple magic, but her side was definitely winning. Elf after elf plunged beneath the water to be devoured by great creatures of the deep or to drown in the crush of spelled eddies.

Wind roared, and suddenly, the Elven Queen lifted from the water, her golden hair dark from the sea and her magic blazing. Moving like an orchestra's conductor, she forced the wind at the spinning columns, and the water evaporated into the sky in bright droplets. Then she faced Astraea.

"Queen Astraea, why must you destroy the balance of

the world?" the Elven Queen said in the language of the sea, her accent wispy and haunting.

Astraea spat the bitter taste of raw air from her mouth and uttered a spell to help her shout back to the Elven Queen. "You give aid to those who would destroy my kynd. Speak not to me about balance! There has been no balance since the birth of the Lapis clan. I seek to set the world to rights, blanketed in ocean water and peaceful for those who deserve such a life. Now, die, and leave me to my quest."

Pointing her scarlet coral spear at the Elven Queen and raising a sheen of water over herself like a bridal veil, Astraea shouted a spell that would leave no trace of this upstart.

"Take her, Sea,
Rip her, Ocean,
Flay and salt her until there's no more to see."

Perched on a floating and gnarled branch, ragged leaves surrounding her like dead fish, the Elven Queen spun, hair flying, and threw a flashing orb at Venu. He disappeared beneath the waves, but the orb gave chase and Astraea could just barely see his body jerk in pain as the light exploded over his face, surely blinding him.

Astraea's spell hit the foaming water eddying around the Elven Queen. The sea heaved. A sound like one thousand crashing waves rushed across the peninsula, then the water grabbed the Elven Queen and dragged her under.

A frenzy of sharks, called by Astraea's spell work, flew through the waves toward the Elven Queen.

Astraea's heart whirled inside her chest, her eyes bright.

The Elven Queen's hand broke the roiling surface as

wine-dark blood billowed around her body. The sharks slithered out to sea. Pieces of torn flesh and lengths of the Elven Queen's hair floated on the glistening waves.

And another of Astraea's enemies, another being who might try to suppress her, to beat her down, was gone. Just like that. The Sea Queen had suffered not a cut nor a bruise.

The sea enveloped Astraea, and she joined her army to celebrate the beginning of the end.

Next, she would take down every last Lapis dragon on the island.

CHAPTER NINETEEN

Vahly had to put a hand to the wall to steady herself. "Arc! The egg. It's hatching."

Bow slung across his body, he raked the vines away and rushed inside, eyes wide. With a whisper and flurry of gestures, he formed a light orb and held it over the egg.

The shell snapped. Another crack appeared, an uneven line between a cluster of dark speckles.

Vahly felt like a youngling at Frostlight, unable to stand the suspense and breathless with anticipation about a forthcoming gift. Arc took her fingers in his.

A wet wing struggled from the crack, steely feathers plastered against pale flesh.

The invisible link between Vahly and the creature emerging from the egg pulled taut. Vahly gasped, chest tightening and blood rushing in her ears. She gripped Arc's hand, but neither spoke. It was as if this moment required the quiet reverence of a holy sacrament. The cave's walls seemed to lean in to observe, their solid presence a comfort.

Jerky movements inside the egg rolled it to its side. A beak the dusky blue of the roses that grew at the northernmost end of Lapis territory poked through the spotted shell. With a rocking motion, the creature managed to free one damp, fuzzed—and rather meaty—paw. Claws extended from the little toes, then retracted.

Vahly's gaze darted from beak to paw to wing, desperate to get a full image of the gryphon.

Arc's lips parted, and he whispered something in elvish. "He is going to be big." A mother's pride beat inside Vahly heart. "When dragon younglings are born with large talons—"

There was a loud snap, and the egg broke fully into halves.

The gryphon uncurled from the pieces to stand on four slightly shaky lion paws. Wings spread wide, the little thing only had peach fuzz where fur and feathers would later sprout. Viridescent eyes locked onto Vahly.

The gryphon let out a plaintive screech.

Vahly's blood drummed, earth magic keening through her, begging her to go to him.

Raw with chaotic emotions, she knelt beside the gryphon. She was confused at why she felt so connected to a creature that wasn't human or dragon or anything she'd ever encountered. Then the incredible devotion and the full knowledge she would protect this small being from anything and everything—and sacrifice everyone and anyone to do it—shocked her to the core. The awe swelling inside her soul bewildered her.

Magic shimmered off the gryphon like it did from Arc, an intoxicating presence that drew one in. But where Arc's presence struck a hot attraction in Vahly, the gryphon's magic made Vahly feel like she had well and truly become a mother.

"I knew you'd hatch, my little friend. I am here, and I am yours." Vahly took a piece of dried meat from Arc's outstretched hand—the Horse Lord knew his way around simplebeasts—and she fed the gryphon, who nibbled sweetly from her trembling palm. His beak clicked across her skin, never injuring, just quick and clean.

When the gryphon finished the tidbit, it hopped closer and looked up into Vahly's face, its beak brushing her nose. It screeched again, and she jumped, a laugh escaping her.

"We need to hunt for you, don't we?" Vahly touched the gryphon's fuzzy, rose-gray head. He was soft and very warm. She turned to Arc. "Nix is going to love him."

"She would have to. She loves you, and this is your familiar."

"How exactly is this all happening?"

Arc looked toward the cave's opening, toward the sea. "I think if we hadn't been attacked, we would have found the answers in Bihotzetik. I know very little."

The gryphon crawled into Vahly's lap, shut its huge eyes, and began breathing, deep and slow. It had fallen asleep. Vahly shook her head, unbelieving at its immediate trust.

"He should've chosen you, Horse Lord." She remembered how the horses at Illumahrah nickered at Arc. "You know about dealing with animals."

"You don't deal with them. You befriend them. You respect them. But I don't have to tell you that. You're already acting as though you know exactly what such a relationship entails."

Vahly waved his comments away, feeling shy about the whole thing. "He is adorable."

"Quite." Arc winked, and Vahly was fairly certain her heart couldn't handle any more happiness.

If Xabier wasn't hurt, the day would have been one of her best. Maybe Xabier would surprise all and live through the heinous attack. He was strong and young. Helena would be there, and perhaps Cassiopeia would send her healers from Illumaharah over to help out as well now that the peace was somewhat secure between the elves and the Lapis.

Nix entered the cave, grinning widely in her human-like form. "Well, what do we have here? This does cheer me up." She had come home empty-handed from hunting, which was unusual for her or any dragon for that matter.

The gryphon raised its head and sniffed the air. He cocked his eaglet head and narrowed his eyes distrustfully. Nix flared her wings and blew a puff of smoke.

"Nix," Vahly chided. "He just hatched. He isn't being impertinent."

Nix raised a scaled eyebrow. "Never too early to put younglings in their place."

But as Nix neared Vahly, the gryphon jumped from Vahly's lap and stood. With a screech of warning, he reared up, pawing the air as his featherless wings flapped.

Nix grinned. "Settle down, youngling. I won't harm your queen." Nix reached forward and plucked the gryphon up in one sapphire-amethyst hand. With a smile, she endured his clawing and the clips of his beak. "Shh."

She ran a finger down his back, then set her other hand on Vahly's shoulder. "You see, little one? We're all on the same side."

The gryphon blinked at Vahly as if asking if this dragon spoke the truth or if he should do his level best to put up a fight.

"Nix is our friend, gryphon." Vahly had to laugh. It was all so ridiculous. She was the worst choice for a mother. She'd teach the creature how to break every rule before the fellow even had his feathers or fur.

Arc stood with his arms crossed, making his thinking face and tapping his lip with his thumb.

"What is tumbling around in your head, alchemist?" Vahly poured water into a dip in the rocky ground. The gryphon lapped it up, splashing water everywhere.

"I wonder if the gryphon will need to see a hierarchy within our small pride here," Arc said. "Gryphons have prides. They fight for leadership. The arrangement of duties and positions leads to higher birth rates and longer lives. For us, I think it would ease the gryphon's stress levels. We might need to establish our hierarchy and demonstrate it to him."

"I am no gryphon." Nix's eyebrow twitched. "You just try to show me you're the alpha, dear Arcturus, and see how much of that gorgeous hair of yours you get to keep."

Arc didn't add tinder to her spark. He walked up to Vahly and kissed her sweetly on top of her head.

Her heart tripped over itself. "What was that for, Ar—"

The gryphon's low screeching-snarl cut her off. He rushed Arc and dug his front claws into Arc's boot, then the gryphon latched onto the black leather with his beak and shook his head hard.

"It's like he is trying to bite your leg off," Vahly said, her words tangled by a surprised laugh. The gryphon was defending her. It was endearing and a bit frightening.

"This is cute now," Arc said, "but when he is full grown in twenty-four hours, this will be a matter of life or death. He would kill me now if he had the means. He may very well try to maim me if he remembers this incident as he matures."

Nix held up a hand. "I have several questions."

"You're not alone." Vahly put a hand to her forehead. "You said he'll mature in a day?"

"That's what I've read. Gryphons are simplebeasts, yes, but they do react to magic unlike many other animals. There is a reason that cathedral showed you a red gryphon, highlighted above all other creatures."

"Showed me?"

"Your magic led you there. You were meant to see that. The cathedrals held earth magic. That is why the floods hadn't entirely decimated the interior and you could have sat upon a bench as if the disaster had been a gentle thing."

"That makes sense. But back to the gryphon. You think we need to do some sort of who-is-the-alpha-here activity with the gryphon to make certain he doesn't decide to eat your head off tomorrow morning at breakfast because you kissed me?"

"That is the basic idea, yes."

Nix crossed her arms. "I had thought you were different from other elves. But here you are, demanding that you're the wisest and must be alpha. Such an elf thing to do."

"I don't care to be alpha. You're welcome to take the role. Vahly, you are the obvious choice, seeing as we both already swore allegiance to you."

"I don't want to be the queen of everything, but it seems like this is my lot in life. I'm going to have to call the moves when we fight because my magic is what is supposedly going to free us. So I'll be the alpha. No jokes, Nix. I hate this, and you know it."

Nix held up her hands. "I said nothing." She sidled over to Arc, who was still permitting the gryphon to eat his boot. "If we don't do something quickly, the elf will be less one piece of footwear." She bent to eye level with the gryphon. "Good job, youngling. If only you had fire."

Vahly sighed. "So how we do show the gryphon our standing in our pride?"

"First, we must decide who will be second and who will be third." Lowering his chin, Arc glanced at Nix. "Now, you won't like this, but..." He pursed his lips. "I hate to be indelicate, but I think at some point I may...touch Vahly if she wishes it. In that case, I must be her second or the gryphon will defend her at the cost of my life and quite possibly his own."

Shaking her head, Nix's gaze flattened. "Here it is. You act at being the cool-headed male of study and serious strategy, but you are truly enjoying yourself, aren't you, Arcturus?" She huffed. "Royalty." She dusted one of her wings, then lay on the ground, one hand slung over a voluptuous hip. "Well, come on. You'll need to lay your teeth on my neck if I'm not mistaken. Let's get this over with." Lifting her chin, she exposed the jewel-toned scales underneath.

"Are you all right with this, Nix?" Vahly asked. "Be honest. I'll find another way to raise this gryphon if you aren't."

"I've done stranger things to help out a couple, my dear." She chuckled, and Vahly heard a touch of the old Nix in the sound.

Vahly sighed, relieved, and picked up the furious gryphon as Arc went to her.

He knelt, his gaze solemn. The wind teased the loose strands of his hair. "Forgive me for this, Mistress Nix of the Dragon's Back."

"Honey tongue. Hmm. If you tire of Vahly, do look me up."

Vahly rolled her eyes.

Arc bent, parted his lips, and set his teeth on Nix's throat. Nix murmured something wildly inappropriate. Vahly growled.

Tucked into the crook of Vahly's arm, the gryphon looked from them to Vahly.

Vahly forced herself to calm down and pet the gryphon as if this were all perfectly normal. The gryphon squeaked and nuzzled her arm.

Arc stood, then helped Nix up. She took his hand and blew a small flame over his head. He jumped, laughing, and bowed slightly.

"And now," he said, eyeing Vahly, "you need to dominate me."

Vahly swallowed hard. A shiver danced down her body.

Nix, wearing a smile loaded with innuendo, took the gryphon from her gently.

"Shut it," Vahly barked.

"I didn't say a thing." Nix stepped away.

Arc knelt as he had after Cassiopeia's crowning, when he had sworn fealty to Vahly. He threw his head back and shut his eyes. His lashes were sable-black against his luminous cheeks. Here was an elven royal exposing his throat to a human. Vahly took a deep breath. This was insanity.

Vahly's body warmed as she regarded him, so strong and so open to her. She imagined what it would feel like to drape herself over him now and have her way with that mouth of his.

But she pushed those thoughts away and went to work, setting her teeth against the cool column of his neck, as he had with Nix.

Arc's throat moved. His breath snagged, then resumed at a quick pace. A tingling spread through Vahly, simmering under her skin like a wildfire spreading through dry grass. His elven magic combined with a power simpler than all of that—desire. She dared to touch the end of her tongue to his skin.

Blushing, she drew away.

"And that's that," she said, her voice husky. "What say you, gryphon? Do you agree not to tear him apart if he deigns to touch me again?"

Arc stood slowly and rubbed the back of his neck. He cleared his throat, then finally looked up. Vahly wasn't certain whether he had enjoyed her secret touch or if he was angered. She decided to pretend it had been an accident.

Nix brushed the gryphon's back. "He is already sprouting feathers and fur. Do I need to set my teeth to his throat now?" She looked as though she worried Vahly might draw her sword at the suggestion.

"I guess so."

Flipping the gryphon gently, Nix kept an eye on the gryphon as she lowered her mouth to his neck. The gryphon's gaze locked on Vahly and she smiled, hoping the intention would be clear. He stilled and stayed that way until Nix finished and turned him upright again.

In awe, Vahly watched the gryphon as Nix set him on the cave floor beside her bed of bright, leafy moss.

The gryphon began smoothing the start of some feathers above his shoulder. Foggy-white fur caught the light, lengthening and thickening from the spot where new feathers stopped and on down his body. Then he hopped out of the cave, ducking the scalloped tips of the akoli grapevines and heading into the sun.

Heart light, Vahly strapped her sword onto her belt and followed.

Nix and Arc chatted behind her.

As Vahly stared at the gryphon, a part of her heart, a corner she had never noticed, opened wide.

Tears pricked her eyes, and she blinked, confused at the sudden and overwhelming emotion. She didn't even know what to name it, but she knew one thing for sure: Even in the most serious of card games, she'd never be able to hide her love for this creature.

Vahly grimaced, her stomach twisting.

A weakness, that's what this was. A chink in her armor. Armor she'd donned after losing Dramour, Ibai, and Kemen.

The gryphon grew another few inches and boasted a

fine lion's pelt. Short and almost wooly, but thinner than wool. Finer, too. His tail swished, the end showing a tuft of hair as the fellow pranced around Vahly. His four paws, bright as gold coins, bounced lightly on the ground.

Magic thrummed inside Vahly's chest, strong and sure. He was a weakness.

But he was also—somehow—a strength.

She exhaled and bent to place hands on either side of the gryphon's head. Sharp intelligence sparked from his eyes, showing a deep wisdom that countered the fact that he had hatched only moments ago.

A strange feeling burned its way from Vahly's palms toward her heart.

Love? Energy? Both?

"What should I call you?" Her voice broke on the last word, overcome with the fact that there was now a being in the world whose life mattered far more than anyone else's.

Vahly chided herself. Amona deserved this feeling from her. Nix too. Possibly even Arc.

But there was no denying it. Though the gryphon was new to the world and to Vahly, her love for him was mighty.

"Familiar." The word glowed in her mind's eye. "We are bonded. We are kin."

Arc and Nix stepped close, smiling and watching the gryphon with undisguised curiosity.

"Humans always did love their animals," Nix said.

The gryphon extended his wings and flew into Vahly's arms, eliciting a surprised yelp from her.

Nix grumbled. "We'll have to work on your takeoff, youngling."

The gryphon's cool beak nudged Vahly's collarbone, then nipped at the tie of her linen shirt. His body warmed her arms and torso, chasing off the day's unusual chill.

"Anyone have suggestions on how to name a gryphon? Arc? You were presumed extinct as this fellow was. Do you have any ideas?"

"I don't see how that relates, but ..." He chuckled. The dawn's light sparkled off his throwing knives. "I suppose you could name him after an attribute he displays."

"You can't speak telepathically with him, can you?"

"It doesn't seem so."

Vahly was secretly glad, though she knew it was churlish to think that way.

Nix's gaze was distant, her mouth turned down, and the joy of the gryphon's hatching gone from her face.

Vahly's heart ached. The old Nix would have made several humorous attempts at names, but grief was pulling at her vivacious spirit, and Vahly wasn't sure it was right to force her to act like she used to. If Nix gave any sign of wanting to talk about their lost ones, Vahly would be there. But she wouldn't push. Not yet.

At least Nix mentioned Dramour, Ibai, and Kemen now and then. That was a start.

If Vahly were being honest with herself, she would admit that she had little desire to express her own ongoing grief. Because what good would it do? They had mourned their friends. The three dragons were gone. Remembering too much only brought searing pain. And that was another weakness, another chink in the armor.

"What do you think the gryphon can do to help our

Queenie girl?" Nix stretched one wing to block the direct sunlight from the squinting hatchling.

Then Nix's gaze caught on something in the distance.

Her eyes opened wide.

Without a sound, she soared into the sky to crash into a snarling Jade dragon.

CHAPTER TWENTY

Vahly held her breath, grabbing the gryphon and spinning.

The leader of the band of rogues blew dragonfire at Nix. She dodged the flame, spinning in the air, her red hair flying as she slashed him across the face. Then the rest of the rogues flew in around them.

Vahly's stomach turned. They must have found the body of the dragon Vahly had killed. The feigned rockslide must not have convinced them, and now, they were set on avenging their fellow rogue.

Baz yowled from the sky as Vahly perched the gryphon on her shoulder to free her hands. She unsheathed her sword, and the familiar weight of the weapon brought an idea to mind.

Magic drumming through her blood, she flipped the blade to draw the edge along the ground.

Arc shouted spells in the elven tongue as he wielded crackling beams and luminous spheres of air magic. The resulting wind forced the dragons back, the smaller wings of their human-like forms shuddering.

Gathering close, they fired on him, and storm clouds clustered above, silver streaks of lightning attracted to their joined power.

Vahly, sweating and chilled, lifted her earth-crusted sword.

By the Source, let this work.

The undeniable urge to move and shout coursed through her, shoving her into action, despite the fact that she didn't know what her magic could do.

The gryphon shrieked at her ear and leapt from the perch of her shoulder. His feathers lengthened as he landed, and she realized he was larger too, standing at the height of Vahly's knee.

One command flashed through her mind. "Fight!" Her voice was hoarse, but the sound carried, earth magic grinding and pounding through the noise.

The gryphon spread its wings, and two shapes crawled from the dirt—gryphons with bodies and legs of dark brown earth, born of the bond between Vahly's magic and the gryphon's inner spirit. Her familiar had indeed changed everything. The realization beat against her heart, in time with the earth, as wings of vines and emerald oak leaves wove themselves into existence, and claws and teeth of briar thorns showed at paw and mouth.

Shaking, Vahly tore her eyes away from the two earthen gryphons to grab a handful of the earth at her feet. She thrust the dirt forward. The earth answered her call. A mound surged upward between the other rogues and Arc, creating a wall of protection around which Arc could launch his spells.

Turning, Vahly watched as the two earthen gryphons flanked the real gryphon, and then surrounded Baz, flying quick to avoid Nix's coordinated attacks on the rogue, and doing their own striking with jagged claw swipes and gnashing at ears and eyes.

Lightning flashed out of a bank of fierce clouds in an otherwise blue sky.

Luc rushed to back up Baz. He blew dragonfire at the gryphons, and a panicked sweat broke across Vahly's face.

The two earth gryphons disintegrated into nothing.

Gutted, Vahly shouted, and the earth lifted her on a wave of sandy dirt, akoli vines, and grasses. Rising up eye-to-eye with Luc, she swung her sword and cut the dragon deeply across one wing. Spraying blood, he reeled back, his body disappearing down the hill and into the rocks at the sea's edge.

Baz reached for the gryphon and grabbed it by the neck. "You seem to like this one, human. I liked Fedon, and you buried him, covering your tracks as if I'd never know a true rockslide from a created one. I have lived here in the wilds while you've been suckling at the Lapis matriarch's teats like a babe! You'll never defeat the Sea Queen. Give up. And don't follow us, or we'll exact more than a life for a life." He held the gryphon high and laughed, moving his talons around the gryphon's neck.

"I will slaughter you, rogue!" Vahly's throat was raw, and her eyes burned.

She stumbled, pulse knocking against her teeth. Pain

dragged across her stomach and just beneath her heart, in the place where her magic guided her.

As he gripped the gryphon and flew higher, Vahly felt the pain in her own neck, only an echo of the hurt the gryphon had to be feeling, but the sensation strangled her enough to stop her voice from working. She pointed her earth-crusted sword at Baz, but no more earth gollums rose.

Baz slashed out at Nix and scored her eye. Vahly tensed, frozen.

Nix fell out of the sky, tucking her wings and rolling to a stop beside the cave.

"Rogues!" Baz waved an emerald hand, his other talons still wrapped around the struggling, mewling gryphon.

Vahly threw her sword onto the mound she'd called up and gripped the dirt. "Swallow!"

The ground under Baz lifted into the sky, ten—now twenty—feet. *Go down, monster. Go down.* Vahly seethed, her nails cutting into her flesh. But the dragon evaded the wave of churning earth and flew up and up, into the mountains, his cohorts trailing him like storm clouds.

Shaking with fury, Vahly ran to Arc. He was bent at the waist and breathing heavily. Smoke drifted from his surcoat, and the odor of burning hair marred his usual natural scent. Nix rushed toward them, hand cupping her eye. Blood leaked from the wound like liquified rubies between her sapphire talons.

Vahly wanted to run screaming—to wreck everything in the world to get her gryphon, but her heart also ached for Arc and Nix. "Are you all right? Did they burn you badly? Nix, how is that eye?"

Arc lifted his left arm. Dragonfire had bubbled the flesh on the tender underside of his upper arm, where he'd evidently raised his hand to block his face. The skin was an angry scarlet. Vahly took his elbow and blew gently on the burn as if that might help. "Can I do anything to help you heal?"

"I'll be fine."

Nix took her hand away from her eye and tried to blink. Blackened blood covered her lid and crusted her eyelashes. Her lips quirked into a sad grin. "I thought it might be fitting to take up Dramour's style. He always said I'd look good in a patch. More mysterious."

Vahly hugged Nix hard, tears threatening. "You'll be even more irresistible."

"By the Blackwater, I wish those rogues would mind their own business," Nix hissed, pulling back and shaking her head.

Shuddering, Vahly closed her eyes and took three deep breaths. "Did you see what the gryphon did with my earth magic?"

"I did." Arc eyed Vahly's fallen sword, then her face. He retrieved the weapon, wiped it clean with his surcoat, then presented it to her across his palms with his head bowed. "And you will use that new magical bond to rescue him with us at your back."

Nix blew a blast of fire into the sky. "Just tell me when."

"Now. That's when. Right now." Vahly ran in the direction the rogues had flown.

Arc ran beside her, eyes fierce and magic curling around his head.

Mid-takeoff, Nix transformed into full dragon form, not

bothering to disrobe and ripping her clothing to pieces that fell from her like ash.

The back of her neck prickling in warning at what they were about to do, Vahly attempted to speak to the gryphon like Arc did to horses.

We are coming for you, my new friend. We will never stop fighting for you.

No answer whispered through her mind. Either he could not communicate in that manner, or he had been silenced.

Vahly ran faster.

CHAPTER TWENTY-ONE

Vahly and Arc rushed up the animal trail, their pace devouring the distance between the rogues and them. Nix flew above, the scent of her fire magic strong in the breeze.

The link between Vahly and the gryphon fell slack—like a fishing line broken and unwinding from its reel—and Vahly's stomach dropped. Her feet gave out and she began to collapse, but Arc took her arms.

"What is it?" He cradled her face in his warm hands as Nix landed behind him, her face full of questions.

Vahly couldn't breathe. If they had hurt him, or worse... *The tie between the gryphon and me...something is wrong. Very wrong.*

Do you think they returned to that same camp? Sweat glistened along Arc's smooth forehead as he helped Vahly begin running again.

With a sensation like a violent jerk, Vahly's magic reminded her of what she already felt deep in her bones—

the exact location of her familiar. "The bond between us is telling me where they've taken him. To their camp."

Snarling, Nix took off into the sky with two heavy beats of her wings. *They will suffer for this. I promise you that, Queen Vahly.* She soared high, then dove to slide through the air directly over Vahly and Arc.

Vahly's hair blew into her face, and the wind of Nix's wings flattened the surrounding salt cedar bushes and scattered their blooms. Nix's full dragon body tore through the wind and ice-blue sky like a storm cloud. Shoving her hair from her mouth, Vahly pummeled the ground with her boots as she sprinted, her whole body shaking and images blinking through her mind.

The gryphon screaming.

Baz ripping the creature's head from its body, blood spraying and bones shining.

Vahly's jaw ached from clenching her teeth and from a lack of oxygen. She pulled a long breath, doing her level best to keep up with an elf and a flying dragon.

Did you realize we are all talking telepathically? Arc asked.

Vahly tripped on an olive tree root but caught herself quickly. They were speaking through thoughts. *I wonder if it has to do with my bond with the gryphon.*

Nix swooped low. *Whatever it is, I'll take it. Let's use it to our advantage, hmm? I'll speed past the rogues, then blast them from behind.*

Vahly swallowed and loosened her shirt's tie, even though it wasn't tight against her neck. *Watch out for the gryphon.*

Of course.

And Arc, will you focus on securing the gryphon? Vahly

asked. *I'll distract the rest. Your air magic is more reliable, and you can control your strikes to keep from hurting the gryphon.*

Arc nodded as they hefted themselves over the boulders so they could take the rogues from above.

Vahly jumped into a circle of seven human-like rogues—Baz was missing—and scattered them as she drew the sword Amona had given her so long ago. Sweat slicked the ivory hilt, but she didn't pause. Rage ringing in her ears and magic sluicing through her veins, she drew the blade across the face of the first dragon to attack her—Roke. Righteous indignation had taken Vahly, and no guilt burdened her soul. Roke's hands went to his ravaged face. He tripped backward and stumbled into the fire, knocking smoking logs through the clearing.

Nix blew dragonfire at Luc and three others, then she struck out and managed to gouge Luc with her immense back talons, digging deep into his groin. He dropped, dead before he hit the ground. Arc cast bright orbs at Tadeo and another dragon, and they howled, most likely temporarily blinded.

Baz had the gryphon tied loosely to a holm oak, like a horse to a tether. The rope, knotted tightly like a noose, was nearly hidden at the neck beneath the gryphon's new feathers and fur.

Vahly's chest seemed to cave in as their bond screamed, and she gasped, pressing a fist against her ribs.

Three times larger than he had been when taken, the gryphon flew left and right, evading Baz's blasts of dragonfire. Baz laughed at the gryphon, then turned and blew a torrent of fire at Arc.

Vahly flipped her sword to cut up and under Tadeo's wing. The blade severed the joint completely.

Tadeo shifted into full dragon form as he shrieked. He lunged, fire roaring from his jagged maw.

Moving faster than she ever had, Vahly cut the ground with her sword, lifted the sandy blade to block the rippling flames, and commanded the earth to rise.

The ground shook.

Magic pounded Vahly's ears and heart, and everyone still alive fell to the quaking earth, unable to stand as trees shook branches onto the ground and cracks cut through the grasses to break the camp into a maze of broken dirt. Vahly swallowed and prayed she wasn't about to accidentally kill her friends. The rogues' eyes went wide, mouths open to breathe fire. The earth lifted Vahly to standing as she shot a look at Arc, willing him to free the gryphon.

Arc hoisted himself up and threw a knife. The silver blade slashed the gryphon's tie.

Her chest tightened with power, her magic longing to speak death. "Destroy!"

The gryphon dove for Baz—the unshifted dragon lay on the ground, dazed by Vahly's earthquake. The gryphon's razor-sharp beak pierced the dragon's exposed throat, then clamped down. The gryphon shook his prey, and Baz's neck snapped. He flopped in the gryphon's hold.

An olive tree, a holm oak sapling, and salt cedar slipped into the earth, as if pressed by an invisible hand. After threading into the sandy mud, the trees erupted from the ground, each in the form of the gryphon, free from their roots and creeping toward Vahly's enemies. A sound like cracking branches poured from the earthen creatures' mouths and sent a shiver down Vahly's back.

The rogues who remained alive—four in total—seemed to realize their leader was lost. Fear ate the wild confidence from their features.

They blew fire at the earth gryphons.

Flames swallowed the salt cedar gryphon, and its remains grabbed the wind and flittered away. The other two earthen gryphons flew over and under the blazing tongues of heat before racing toward the rogues.

Circling the rogues, Nix flashed a straight, focused line of fire at the largest dragon's back.

He spun to return the favor, but the olive tree gryphon flew at his neck and took his spine in a flash of glistening nettle teeth that had to be strong as steel to do the damage they did.

The olive and oaken gryphons turned to face Vahly. For direction? With a grunt, she pointed her sword at the last three rogues, and the gryphons—the true familiar included—rushed the enemy dragons and attacked in a horror of blood, leaves, twisting roots, claws, and rioting feathers.

Silence blanketed the air.

The last rogue's emerald face paled as the wind grabbed the earthen gryphons and broke them apart into nothing.

Vahly's legs folded beneath her, and she hit the ground hard. Blood oozed from her earlier head wound. Her sword arm throbbed with the burn of dragonfire. She fell forward, palms to the earth, her bones clacking like an old woman's.

A soft head nuzzled under her arm, and a beak as smooth as a river rock touched her cheek. She lifted her eyes and smiled, drawing the gryphon closer. The gryphon stared with eyes that were both innocent and wise, reminding her of Etor—Arc's horse that had been missing since the day Arc had headed into the marshes to help her.

Nix and Arc collapsed beside them.

Arc pushed sweat-slicked hair away from his face. Two lines of dark blood ran down from his pointed ears. Nix remained in full dragon form. Her snout pressed against Vahly's back. The gryphon glanced at Nix, then at Arc. Arc nodded at the gryphon, telling him to allow the contact with Vahly.

Vahly shook her head, unbelieving. Her own band of breakers was developing new habits to support its tiny culture of misfit fighters. She put a hand on Nix's cheek as Nix settled onto all fours behind her and Arc.

I'm sad that Roke had to go. Nix licked a wound that leaked from a spot between her front talons. *But time could not be spared to speak with him.*

Vahly's temples pounded. She hated that kill, too. He might have been talked onto their side, but the violence had escalated so quickly. It had been Roke or her familiar and—

An image materialized in Vahly's mind, separate from her own thoughts.

She froze, watching as an imaginary Roke spoke to a nearly transparent Baz and Luc. The young dragon nodded and smiled, his form hazy like a plume of smoke. He turned, and there was a deer beside their campfire, its body trembling as it died. He smiled and tended the fire, not bothering to mercy kill the simplebeast like he should have, showing no respect for the creature at all.

The illusion faded.

Vahly blinked at Arc and Nix. *Did you see that too?*

Nix's long neck stretched, her crystalline spikes sparkling, and then she cocked her head at the gryphon, giving him a questioning look. *Was that you, youngling?* Vahly's heart lifted. *I truly think it was.* She opened her arms, and the gryphon came closer, allowing her to hug him tightly. He smelled like bruised herbs and animal musk.

Arc's deep voice massaged Vahly's mind. *The gryphon's ability to communicate turns this band into a proper battle unit.*

Vahly stroked the gryphon, whose back end couldn't fit in her lap. His lion tail flicked the bloodied ground. She was too exhausted to say more, to do more.

As Arc healed Vahly's head and Nix's wound, Arc and Nix began a good-natured argument about the ins and outs of what the gryphon's power would mean and how it had intensified with his ongoing growth.

The gryphon himself overwhelmed Vahly. She ran a hand along the rose-gray feathers that cloaked his stout neck. They were soft and fitted perfectly, like layered ovals in a game board.

The gryphon clicked its beak, cooing at her touch, his head already well above her own as he grew second by second, little by little. His presence relaxed Vahly and helped her accept the atrocities as a horror that could not be avoided. Here was one creature Vahly would never con and never wanted to.

Vahly gasped as the gryphon opened his mind to her and showed images of her battling the rogues, her face fierce and determination like a brand on her features. Somehow, through the bond, she could feel his respect for her. His dedication hummed like a song, haunting her heart with a love that was new but felt ancient.

The gryphon's name bloomed inside Vahly's head. The urge to speak it pinched at her throat.

The gryphon nudged Vahly, then he stood on all four lion paws, gaze piercing her.

"The gryphon's name is Kyril."

Nix hoisted herself up and roared in approval.

Giving Kyril a playful smile, Arc bowed. "A pleasure to know you."

Kyril flashed an image of the sky through Vahly's head, then he bent low, at her feet, edging his wing out of the way.

Nix bumped Vahly's back. *Is this another show of submission?*

Vahly blinked and flexed her hands. *He wants me to fly with him.*

Arc stepped closer, rubbing his hands together. "Well, go on!" he said aloud, his excitement apparently making him forget to use telepathy. "And test your magic with him while you're aloft. Perhaps you'll discover a new way to fight the sea folk."

"Easy for you to say, elf. You aren't the one who'll be dragged through the heavens. I have to think about this."

Nix snorted and pawed the ground. *Get on the gryphon, Vahly.* Nix's lemon eyes examined Kyril. *He's your soul mate or whatever. He isn't going to drop you. That's insulting to a flyer, honestly. Don't even bring it up.*

"My familiar."

Nix growled.

"All right. Fine. I'll go up. But you're coming along and taking Arc with you."

Arc's eyes widened. He stilled his hands and looked from Vahly to Nix, tentative hope tugging at his features. Dragons did not allow anything to "ride" them.

Vahly snorted. "After all we've been through, surely you don't care about the old conventions, do you, Nix?"

We would have an edge in the air. I realize that, Nix said. *But how is he supposed to sit on my back with all these spikes?*

"If I may," Arc said, leaning closer to Nix at her nod. He studied the space behind her neck and between her wings. "I do think I would find a seat just there." His hand indicated a narrow spot behind one of the mid-sized spines and a row of lesser spikes.

Well, I once dressed as a male to get into a competing smuggler's hoard inside the city of thieves. This can't be much worse than that degradation.

You really hate trousers, don't you? Vahly said.

I don't mind the type we wear under dresses, with the fine lace and the silken details. Do not judge me, darling. I'm a female, and I love being a female. I'm a proud dragon, and I love being a proud dragon. I must weigh the costs of straying from who I am. The vertical slits inside her eyes opened wide, then narrowed, evaluating Arc and most likely imagining how it would feel to fly with a burden between her wings.

Then she lowered her head and shifted her wing.

Arc put a foot on her bent foreleg, then did what Vahly was beginning to think of as an elf-leap. He landed exactly on the spot he'd chosen.

Skin rippling, Nix shook. Arc grasped the spike in front of him to hold on, his hair loose around his face. When Nix settled, Arc beamed at Vahly. The youngling he had been stared out of his ancient eyes.

"Are we ready?" Vahly pressed a hand against Kyril's pelt. Warmth and magic sparked down her arm, sweet and comforting.

She climbed on and straddled Kyril's back. His wings spread wide, fanning into a glorious show of feathers alternately tipped in black and white. Rearing, he nearly threw Vahly off, but she managed to clutch the mane-like fur beneath his neck feathers. Her pulse throbbed, and her hands sweated so much that it was difficult to hang on. She really hoped this wasn't the worst idea they'd had yet.

Jumping at the sky, Kyril lifted off, his wings beating the air as the ground dropped farther and farther away. Both cool air and warm drafts slid across Vahly's cheeks, tangled her hair, and tugged at her clothing. Her smile was so intense that it actually hurt her lips, but of course, she didn't care.

"This is even better than taking all against Aitor!"

Nix flapped her azure wings and rolled one big eye. *You might have a problem, my dear. We will discuss your gambling addiction once you save the world, all right?*

Vahly leaned close to Kyril's head, his feathers tickling her chin and nose. "Can you outfly that obnoxious dragon over there?"

Would he understand her? What if he only—

Kyril ripped Vahly's ponderings right out of her head as he sped up, then dove toward the mottled patches of scrub and grapevines growing along the sloping mountains. Vahly let out a triumphant shout as he veered left, taking a sharp turn toward a cliff face beyond the limits of where Vahly had traveled, farther into Jade territory.

Show off! Nix shouted. *I suppose he doesn't need my lessons. A natural flier!* Her laugh flavored the tone of her voice. *I like him, Queenie! But you tell him the only reason he has the best of me today is because I'm still healing. I'll annihilate him in speed and maneuvering when I'm at my best again.*

Arc's head was turned toward Vahly, and she knew he was analyzing Kyril's every move for later discussion.

The cliff face raced at them.

Kyril? Vahly thought to him. *We might have a chance against the sea folk. Let's not end our lives this quickly, if you don't mind.*

Every crevice came into focus. Closer. Closer. Vahly's heart slammed against her ribs.

"Kyril!"

CHAPTER TWENTY-TWO

R yton sliced the water like a spelled shell knife, the dragonfire burns he'd suffered during his first run-in with the Earth Queen stinging. It was time to stop mulling around the ruins, hoping the Earth Queen would return. He had to use this terrible creature he'd taken on and climb out of the sea. Today.

A shudder tore him, from both the thing on his back and the idea of being above water for an extended length of time.

Zipping through an array of blood-red jellyfish, he reached the gentle rise of rocks that led to the shoreline north of Bihotzetik, a goodly distance from where the Earth Queen and her minions had been last time. He would need to gather himself onshore, to make certain he truly could function on land, before he attempted the killing.

His toes gripped the small rocks, and he slipped, swimming again.

No, I must walk, he chided himself.

His foot slammed against the pebbles and raised whirls

of grit. Head clearing the surface, he took an experimental breath and surveyed the immediate area for signs of life. A few birds flew by, black and raucous, but no larger beasts—human, elf, or dragon—showed themselves. His lip curled at the thought of being so close to his greatest enemy, the murderers of his sister, while he was out of water. Fear lanced his need for revenge, and he realized he was shaking badly.

"You had better work, monster," he hissed at the black creature he carried.

A cough ripped his throat, the raw air burning and scouring. He bent double and put his hands on his knees, and his lungs worked like a dying squid inside his chest. The creature hummed with magic. A bolt of energy surged down his spine.

With a shout, he jerked upright.

Pain trailed the magic, but then the sensation faded. He could breathe properly. Touching his gills, he realized they had reduced in size and lay flat on his flesh as if in hiding. A chill raged over his limbs, and he stumbled, falling to his knees. He froze as his fins diminished in a manner similar to his gills. They remained visible but were less stiff, and their seaweed color faded to match his skin.

Ryton's stomach turned. The change was so much like the dragons' version of transformation, how their wings and talons lessened in size and their scales softened into more elven features. He forced himself to take three deep breaths.

The pebbles of the coastline spilled onto a knoll covered in dry seaweed—no, it was called *grass*. The material scratched at his feet, but not in a harsh way. It was odd, but not painful. It was all so strange. He looked around to see rising mountains, the base of their incline only a short distance away.

Something moved along the shore.

No, it was the rippling shadow of a creature flying.

Blinking furiously, he tried to see the sky, to keep looking up and away, but the harsh white seared his eyes. A headache throbbed between his eyebrows.

Rubbing the pained spot, he searched for cover, head down. He couldn't have the Earth Queen and her minions seeing him before he had a chance to attack.

But there were no caves here. Not one large enough to hide him.

Perhaps farther south... But he could smell the Earth Queen that way. His own camp couldn't be that close.

Camp.

He groaned.

Hopefully, he could end this without having to spend more than a few hours above water.

Pressing onward, dizzier than he'd ever been in his entire life, he found a stand of trees with thick leaves, wide as his two hands side by side. The growth grabbed the sunlight and drowned it, leaving the space under the sporadically spaced limbs blessedly dim.

He collapsed in the midst of the foreign plants.

When his breathing grew regular and his headache faded, he maneuvered himself so he could view the entirety of the coastline. He couldn't yet look to the skies though. His eyes needed more time to adjust.

To keep his frustration tied tight, he rummaged around to discover a rock for sharpening and went to work on his shell spear. Whispering magic, he strengthened the weapon.

When he stretched to set the stone on the ground, a gust of raw air hit his face. He began coughing again, cursing this place for even existing.

Once he murdered the Earth Queen, all of the land and its horrors would be doomed to die when Queen Astraea saw fit. It would be over quickly after that. How could his sister Selene have been so interested in this place? Why had he himself been fascinated with shipwrecks and human oddities? This place was a nightmare, and he would be glad to see its end.

A movement caught Ryton's eye. Some creature shifted a leaf near his foot. The thing leapt from its hiding spot and landed on Ryton's knee.

Ryton froze.

The beast was no bigger than a fist. Two lines ran down its back. A measly tail pointed from its end. As the disgusting thing nibbled what looked like a large seed, its tiny, liquid eyes watched him. He shuddered. Would it bite him? Its mouth was far too small to cause great damage. But what if it was venomous like some sea snakes?

The furred being hopped off his leg without incident before scurrying through the grass.

Ryton released a breath and chided himself yet again. One wee beast and he froze? Was he not the greatest general in the sea? Thank the Source that Grystark hadn't been here to witness that scene. Ryton never would have heard the end of the ribbing.

He watched the creature climb another tree ten feet away. The beast joined two others, and they chittered like old friends. A fourth creature emerged from a tangle of dry seaweed—no, just *weeds*—its form far smaller. A youngling. The furry things nuzzled one another before running into the nest to hide from an osprey's shadow.

The words for above-water life were coming back to him. It'd been many years since his youthful schooling, but the information was there, only needing to be shaken from his streamlined, military mind.

Selene's smiling face blinked behind his eyes. His sister had been top of her class in above-water topics, a frowned-upon yet tolerated subject. One had to know their enemy. Selene had been the youngest to pass the dragon test. Ryton's teeth ground together. Such an irony. Selene had been interested in the very creatures who had burned her to death.

What would she have thought of this mission of his?

If he'd been killed that day instead of her—every day he wished for it—would she be here, hunting the one soul who could keep the dragons and all the land creatures alive? Surely, she would. Wouldn't she?

Ryton grabbed for the sharpening stone again and went to work on his spear just to have something to do with his hands.

Selene's voice echoed through his memory. He could almost hear her in his head.

"Big brother and his brave plans! I wonder what the queen will do with you if you ever do make it into her inner circle. You are far too handsome to ignore. And much too quick for her to dismiss. Perhaps you will be the next queen's consort? If you gain all the immense sway I think you will, you must promise to take me near the coast for an expedition."

Ryton shook his head, and the sharpening stone slipped from his fingers. Pressure built behind his eyes and in his throat. She had been teasing, but she'd stumbled onto the true future.

Ryton had become Astraea's consort and her general. But here was the expedition, and Selene was long dead. Would she have marveled at the furry creatures? Would she have wanted to spy on a dragon?

A sad smile quirked Ryton's lips. He coughed again, throat tight with raw air and raw pain. She would've loved this quest, despite the pain and the fear. Selene had been remarkably tough considering how small she'd been at birth. She had been as squirmy as a little squid when she was an infant. Her face had filled with wonder when Ryton wiggled an eyebrow to entertain her.

Ryton leaned his head back on one of the trees' rough and spindly trunks and let the memories wash over him. She had been taken too soon. Gripping his spear, knuckles straining, he wished he would have acted differently the day she died. He could have come up beside her more quickly. With one change in that day's events, he might have been able to block the dragonfire for a moment and let her escape. One wrong move and he'd lost her.

His spear fell to the ground beside him, and he flexed his hands, hands that had once held a sweet girl. He looked toward the sea and was glad a slim cloud cover blanketed the vicious sun so he could actually focus on the jagged waves of pearl white and soothing blue.

Perhaps Selene watched him now. Perhaps she too wished he'd acted differently that fateful day.

Shaking his head, he pushed the guilt under the sand drifts of time.

Only now mattered.

He couldn't change the past. It was foolish to moan over mistakes made long ago. Now he had the chance to act, to avenge Selene, to destroy the one person who might protect the vicious dragons.

Nothing mattered except assassinating the Earth Queen.

CHAPTER TWENTY-THREE

J ust when Vahly thought this was it, the end, Death raising his scythe, Kyril lifted his head, torqued his wings, and flew in a vertical parallel to the mountain, his paws and belly brushing the cliff.

A laugh pealed out of Vahly. Her legs gripped the gryphon's body as he canted up and over the rounded peak. The wind of their flight rattled a congregation of holm oaks. Kyril jettisoned into the sky, and Vahly closed her eyes, feeling like nothing could stop them now.

She inhaled the scent of the earth far below, its metallic tang of rock and mineral. The musk of animal surrounded Kyril, and her nose could even sense that same hint from the creatures hiding in the clusters of olives and in the caves. Rejecting the scent of the not-too-distant sea, she focused on the earth and the land animals.

Earth magic drummed in her ears, and she felt that same old tug, the sensation that was quickly becoming familiar. The magic brought her gaze up and forced her to look southeast.

The Lapis territory?

A negative sensation pressed her head.

Where did it want her to look? The city of thieves? The cider house? She frowned. It should've been clear to her. This journey toward a power that could fight the Sea Queen wasn't at its end yet. She had more to learn and far greater things to accomplish. If not, the dragons, the elves, and Vahly herself would fall beneath the sea folk's devouring waves.

In her mind, the image of the mosaic in the obsidian cathedral materialized. The gryphon in the center. The four corners that showed the Blackwater spring, a group of familiars, a swaddled infant, and a massive oak. She'd washed in the spring and her power had finally opened its eyes. Now, she had her familiar.

The corners might represent the steps she had to take to come fully into her magic.

Vahly's mouth fell open.

Yes, her magic seemed to whisper. *Go.*

And she knew. The antlers next to the swaddled baby meant she had to visit her birthplace with her familiar. She and Kyril had to venture into the Lost Valley, where her mother had given birth, where her mother had offered her up to Amona.

A rightness suffused Vahly's bones.

The sensation lightened the weight on her shoulders and set her heart into perfect rhythm with the earth's pulsing beat, a sound that never really left her these days. She touched her chest and smiled, the sound and feel of her magic a comfort, strengthening her.

But before they could risk the trip to the Lost Valley, she and Kyril had some Arc-style experimenting to do.

And the earth below was calling, calling, calling.

Summoning every drumming beat of earth magic in her blood, Vahly followed her instincts, didn't question why, and firmly commanded with a word.

"Fly!"

On the ground, in the speeding shadow of both Nix and Kyril, a bank of thick vines tangled into the dirt. An oval boulder boasting quartz that dazzled Vahly's eyes tumbled to meet five more smaller boulders. The rocks smashed the dirt where the vines had disappeared.

Sandy ground exploded.

Vahly couldn't close her gaping mouth at the creature that emerged from the chaos.

A gryphon made of earth magic lifted into the air with a screech that buffeted Vahly's ears. Wings of vine and dirt pushed the air to lift the new gryphon's head of quartz-laden rock, body of rolled and molded stone, and claws and beak of the blackest roots.

A shiver ran over Vahly. She gripped Kyril's scruff.

The earthen gryphon consumed the air and rose to meet them. The magic had used the rock to reproduce a detailed, hooked beak as well as empty and narrowed eye sockets that made Vahly intensely relieved the creation was on her side of things.

With another screech, the earthen gryphon opened its beak. A pointed tongue of braided vines flicked from its mouth.

May I throw air magic at your creation, my queen? Arc's voice was tight with excitement.

Kyril and his double soared high, then swooped low.

Go for it, but I'll be honest, I'm a little scared of my own work here.

Nix huffed, a snorting gust in the rushing winds. *Did you think defeating Queen Astraea would involve simple hoods and a con? You're a true Earth Queen, and we have waited so, so long for you, my lovely. Own it.*

Vahly's trembling fingers knotted the thick fur at Kyril's neck, just under the last of his head's great feathers. Nix stretched her elegant neck and held her chin at a proud tilt as she flew closer to the earthen gryphon.

Arc blasted the earthen gryphon with a glittering sphere of light and dark.

Vahly clenched her teeth. The air magic could injure Kyril. It might turn the earthen beast into something foul.

The magic splashed the created gryphon. Waves of sparkling light and dancing shadows clung to its wings, then flowed over its body, head, and tail of vines.

And then the entire creation disappeared.

Vahly held her breath. *Arcturus. What did you do?*

He hissed something in elvish. *I think it lives still. Please just keep a watch, my queen.*

Vahly wondered if perhaps the magic could be viewed better from the corner of her eye, from indirect focus on the workings, just as it was around Arc's head and hands. She turned her head and watched the place beside Kyril, where the creature had been a moment ago. But she saw nothing.

Until she did.

Tentacles the colors of midnight and noon clasped the earthen gryphon, winding, shimmering, dazzling. But if

Vahly tried too hard to examine the magic, it faded from view.

You camouflaged him! I can see it.

Nice work, alchemist. Nix blew a blast of dragonfire and started to descend. She was probably tiring.

Wait, Nix. Please! Arc shouted. Vahly could see his head bending closer to Nix's ear. *Would you blow more fire toward the earthen gryphon? Just in front of him.*

You'll destroy it, Vahly said. *The rogues used their fire to roast the other creatures we made, or did you forget that nightmare? I wish I could.*

She will aim in front of it, he said. *And I hypothesize my air magic will protect it from destruction. Are you willing to risk it?*

Vahly gave him a nod. *I'll take the gamble. Nix? Are you willing?*

Nix rushed Kyril and Vahly, and then flew straight up, giving them a wink before pouring dragonfire down, exactly in the place Arc had indicated. It wasn't an easy feat, as she had to fly in an odd position, nearly flying backwards. Vahly remembered Amona utilizing the move in a battle near the sea folk's capitol of Tidehame.

Nix's dragonfire broke across the earthen gryphon's beak.

The weave of air magic buffeted the flames like a wall. But they wouldn't be going against fire in the coming fights against the sea folk. Dragonfire was on their side. Vahly was about to suggest they all head back down to rest when a strange sound cracked the air.

The earthen gryphon opened its beak, and emerald fire poured from its mouth to lance the quiet, cerulean sky.

Vahly blinked, unbelieving. Her earthen gryphon had breathed fire.

The combined use of fire, air, and earth magic had brought another fire-breathing creature into life, a being that might fight on their side against the sea.

Tipping its wings in a salute to Vahly, the earthen gryphon roared flames again.

Kyril startled and listed to the right.

Nix lifted higher, but not in time. Her talons scored Vahly's ear, and both pain and blood heated Vahly's face.

Stones, Vahly! I am sorry!

Kyril keened and dropped. Vahly's stomach lurched at the rapid descent as the ground raced at them. The earthen gryphon mimicked Kyril's panic and rushed toward a landing place. But it was traveling too quickly. It would be destroyed on impact.

"It's all right," Vahly said to Kyril, trying to calm him. The wind ripped her words from her mouth. Kyril most likely couldn't even hear her. She tried to speak louder, then repeated the same telepathically. *The fire won't hurt us. It will fight for us. With us.*

Head pounding, palms slick with perspiration, Vahly twisted to see the earthen gryphon plummet and smash into the ground.

Exactly the ending she and Kyril would experience if he didn't shake this panic.

I understand. But I swear on the Source, we're all right. Feel the wind through your feathers, Kyril. We're alive. Let's keep it that way, eh?

Nix and Arc shouted in a jumble of telepathic nonsense. She knew they were right behind her and Kyril.

Kyril flashed images at Vahly. The colors and shapes showed a blurred version of what had just happened.

Vahly took a slow breath and forced herself to smooth a gentle, non-panicked hand over the back of Kyril's head. *Just land us carefully, and I promise you all will be well.*

A shudder rippled beneath Kyril's pelt. He extended his wings and slowed their descent.

Exhaling with relief, Vahly braced herself for the impact, but Kyril's paws greeted the earth without a bump, and Vahly found herself once again safely on land.

Nix touched down beside them, and Arc leapt to the ground, graceful as always.

He held a hand up to help Vahly down. Normally, she would've waved him off with a smile, but Kyril's little death wish adventure had shaken her. She accepted Arc's warm hand, curling her fingers around his. His other hand went to the small of her back. He pulled her close as he helped her down, his body caressing hers. Vahly's breath hitched, stuck in her throat, as she met his dark gaze.

"My queen." His lips quirked into a pleased grin. "That was quite a show."

Green fire! Nix shouted into their heads. *I have never heard of such a thing. Very impressive.* She shook her great head and bared her teeth in a dragon's version of a smile. *I can't wait to plot out how we can use this against the sea monsters. They'll be so surprised! Arcturus, thank you for pushing us to combine our magic up there. Nicely played, elf.*

"We'll need to test the earth fire on sea water as well as flesh and scale."

Nix shuddered, her tail whipping the blooms off a salt cedar.

"Way to ruin the mood." Vahly pinched his side. She reached over his arm to pat Kyril before the gryphon loped to a bunch of grass, where he crouched to hunt some small simplebeast.

"Nothing can ruin this." Arc smiled, his gaze pulling Vahly's attention to him.

She had the urge to kiss him right then and there, to press her mouth on his and celebrate this new magic in the best way.

Fire blazed where Nix had stood, and suddenly, she was in her human-like form.

Vahly started to pull away from Arc, but his hold on her body tightened as if in request. Vahly swallowed as Arc's chest moved against her in a heavy breath.

Nix waved her fingers over her shoulder as she walked away. "I'm going to grab my backup dress while you two take a moment. We created some grand power between us." She disappeared into their cave.

Towering above Vahly and Arc, Kyril tugged a strand of Vahly's hair, his wide eyes pleading. She pressed her palm against his beak, and he cooed. He narrowed his eagle eyes at Arc as if in warning, then turned and followed Nix.

The ocean crashed in the distance, and the chirp of distura birds filled the air.

Arc's tree sap scent tantalized Vahly's nose. The sweep of his hand down her spine heated her better than any fire.

"If you keep that up, elf, I might burst into flames right here. Then where would you be?"

He raised an eyebrow and whispered against her forehead, his breath hot. "So you wish for me to stop?"

Goosebumps ravaged Vahly's arms and sides. "I

suppose I could tolerate it for a few minutes. Though you know we have work to do."

His fingers slid into her hair and mussed the already falling braid. The touch of his fingers turned her joints to pudding, and she fought to retain an ounce of dignity, not certain if he felt as strongly as she did. Perhaps this was just a nice bit of fun for him. It was not so for Vahly. Arcturus, royal elf and alchemist, had become her dear friend. Her confidante. The face she longed to see first each sunrise.

"What is it?" Arc smiled and brushed a thumb over her cheekbone.

"I just realized I'm rather fond of you."

"Just now? I puzzled that out weeks ago."

Vahly nipped Arc's neck. "Don't forget who is alpha over here."

He laughed. "Never, my queen."

His eyes grew serious, the flirtatious gleam fleeing as he pressed one hand against his own heart. It was as if a chill raked him, and for a moment, he paled.

Vahly gripped his surcoat, the cloth bunching. What was happening? "Arcturus?"

He took one of her hands, opened her palm, and traced a symbol there. Magic billowed in smoky plumes of amethyst, lapis lazuli, citrine, and gold.

"Take this spell, Vahly of the Earth. If you use it, it will die, but you will live."

The magic hovered over her palm like a whirlwind. "What is this?" Golden flecks dazzled her eyes with their intensity. Although the spell floated, it weighed down her hand like a sack of coin.

Arc pressed her hands together between his own. The

magical whirlwind disappeared between her palms. "If you're in dire need, if your death shows its face, do the following, and know you will live." He stepped back, put his palms together, then breathed into them. "You must focus on this moment and what the magic looked like to you before it faded. Then the spell will give you your life back."

"This is too much. Is this hurting you in some way? You went white as a moon moth when you gathered the energy to cast this. I'm not going to use a spell that can hurt you."

With a hand, he slapped his chest once. "You can see that I'm hale and healthy. No harm to me, my queen. It is a difficult spell. That is all."

She sighed. "Thank you, Arc. Truly." She poked him in the ribs. "So I'm pretty much immortal now, hmm?" She wiggled her eyebrows. Earth Queens were known to live a very long time regardless, and with this spell...

He grinned. "Unfortunately not. This spell will only work once. And it doesn't always function correctly. You merely took a year from my life."

Vahly's heart seized. She reached for him, then fisted her shaking hand. "Take it back. I can't accept that. Take it back. That's a command. From your queen."

"Apologies." Arc bowed his head. "The spell cannot be undone. I have had many years. I'll have many more, if our plans go well. If not, one year will make no difference."

Vahly's chin dropped, and she stared at Kyril's huge paw print in the sandy dirt beside Arc's black boots. Heart swelling, brightening, she met Arc's gaze. "I'm a smuggler, a liar, a gambler, and at times, a thief. Nonetheless, the Source has rewarded me with you."

"The Blackwater weighed your soul. You are balanced."

Vahly shrugged. "You could come up with a better line than that, couldn't you?" She huffed. "*Balanced.*"

Arc's fingers danced down the side of her neck. Her pulse ticked faster and faster. "Perhaps I should simply show you how I feel." His half-lidded eyes studied her face, his gaze like a touch on her lips, her ear, the hollow of her throat.

Kyril and Nix emerged from the cave with supplies.

Nix's bag dropped to the ground. She shrieked—frozen in terror.

The world tilted.

Arc flew backward, struck by an unseen force.

Kyril galloped toward them.

Before Vahly could even turn to look, arms grabbed her from behind and a cold spear's edge bit her neck and the salty, sour smell of the ocean swamped her nose.

HOLDING THE EARTH QUEEN TIGHTLY, RYTON ANGLED THE spear just under her chin. With one move, one small jab of that sharp steel across her artery, she would be dead, and the war would be over. The dragons could never win without her. Astraea was too powerful.

But then Ryton's gaze drifted over the Earth Queen's messy braid and Selene's voice pierced his mind. A memory of her at eight years of age gripped him. Selene's hair had been braided just like this, chaotic and drifting around her ears.

Memories assaulted him.

"I want to try out the dragon language on dragons,"

young Selene had said long ago, her chin raised defiantly at Ryton. "It would be a real test of what I can do."

He had gone to his knee and grabbed her little arms, panic lashing his heart like a stingray's tail. "Never. They're murderous beasts. Filthy and vicious. Their only true passion is to spill our blood. Are your tutors not explaining the truth to you properly? Perhaps we need to visit and remind them of their duty."

Selene kissed his nose with her tiny lips, then pulled away, a spark in her eyes. "I'm not afraid. And if I could talk to them, maybe they would be nice. You don't know. You never tried."

"Many have tried. And were burned to death for their efforts."

"That was a long time ago. Now is now," she had said with all the ignorance and optimism of youth.

And here Ryton was in the present, with Selene dead and her optimism gone with her. When Ryton slayed this Earth Queen, there would never be another chance for talking as Selene had first wanted to do as a youngling. It would be over. Astraea would reign, and everything here on land—the elves, the small simplebeasts, the mountains and trees—it would all be drowned forever. Gone.

Ryton's killing blow waited.

He could do it now. Return a hero.

Or he could wait.

Just a while. And try to talk to others about the possibilities here, the finality of the whole thing.

It would not hurt to pause, to consider.

He would take her prisoner. Maybe he would kill her tonight. Maybe not.

Arms clenched around the Earth Queen, he leapt backward.

As Vahly was lifted and went soaring over the cliff's edge, she saw three things: Arc's magic flaring, sun-bright and shadowed, chasing them; Nix's dragonfire rippling in time with the ocean's crash; Kyril wailing and taking to the sky.

And then the sea swallowed Vahly and her captor whole, and she knew no more.

Alisha won't keep you waiting long to find out what happens next!
Grab book three in the Dragons Rising series, QUEEN OF SEAS, today!
Have you signed up for Alisha's newsletter for updates, giveaways, and your library of FREE books and bonus material from this series?
Go to https://www.alishaklapheke.com/free-prequel-1 to check that out.

Other books by Alisha Klapheke

Uncommon World Series

Claimed
Waters of Salt and Sin
Fever
Plains of Sand and Steel
Forests of Silver and Secrets

Rune Kingdom

The Edinburgh Seer Trilogy
The Edinburgh Seer
The Edinburgh Heir
The Edinburgh Fate